Two men came in with guns in their hands. One of the guns dug sharply into Dalmas' ribs, and the man who was holding it said urgently: "Back up, and make it snappy. This is one of those stick-ups you read about."

He was dark, good-looking and cheerful. His face was as clear as a cameo, almost without hardness.

He smiled.

The one behind him was short and sandy-haired. He scowled. The dark one said: "This is Walden's dick, Noddy. Take him over and go through him for a gun."

## Four classic stories by the all-time master of detective fiction

"You can't ask for anything better."
*San Francisco Chronicle*

**By Raymond Chandler**
***Published by Ballantine Books:***

**KILLER IN THE RAIN**

**PLAYBACK**

**THE LONG GOODBYE**

**THE SIMPLE ART OF MURDER**

**PICKUP ON NOON STREET**

**TROUBLE IS MY BUSINESS**

**THE LITTLE SISTER**

# RAYMOND CHANDLER

## PICKUP ON NOON STREET

BALLANTINE BOOKS • NEW YORK

The stories in this book appeared in *The Simple Art of Murder*, Houghton Mifflin, 1950. The material in that edition originally appeared in the following magazines: *Black Mask, Dime Detective, Detective Fiction Weekly, The Saturday Evening Post, Atlantic Monthly* and *The Saturday Review of Literature.*

ISBN 0-345-33211-3

This edition published by arrangement with Houghton Mifflin Company

Printed in Canada

First Ballantine Books Edition: July 1972
Seventh Printing: September 1985

Cover art by Whistlin' Dixie

# Contents

# Pickup
# on Noon
# Street

# PICKUP
# ON NOON STREET

THE MAN and the girl walked slowly, close together, past a dim stencil sign that said: Surprise Hotel. The man wore a purple suit, a Panama hat over his shiny, slicked-down hair. He walked splay-footed, soundlessly.

The girl wore a green hat and a short skirt and sheer stockings, four-and-a-half inch French heels. She smelled of Midnight Narcissus.

At the corner the man leaned close, said something in the girl's ear. She jerked away from him, giggled.

"You gotta buy liquor if you take *me* home, Smiler."

"Next time, baby. I'm fresh outa dough."

The girl's voice got hard. "Then I tells you goodbye in the next block, handsome."

"Like hell, baby," the man answered.

The arc at the intersection threw light on them. They walked across the street far apart. At the other side the man caught the girl's arm. She twisted away from him.

"Listen, you cheap grifter!" she shrilled. "Keep your paws down, see! Tinhorns are dust to me. Dangle!"

"How much liquor you gotta have, baby?"

"Plenty."

"Me bein' on the nut, where do I collect it?"

"You got hands, ain't you?" the girl sneered. Her

1

voice dropped the shrillness. She leaned close to him again. "Maybe you got a gun, big boy. Got a gun?"

"Yeah. And no shells for it."

"The goldbricks over on Central don't know that."

"Don't be that way," the man in the purple suit snarled. Then he snapped his fingers and stiffened. "Wait a minute. I got me a idea."

He stopped and looked back along the street toward the dim stencil hotel sign. The girl slapped a glove across his chin caressingly. The glove smelled to him of the perfume, Midnight Narcissus.

The man snapped his fingers again, grinned widely in the dim light. "If that drunk is still holed up in Doc's place—I collect. Wait for me, huh?"

"Maybe, at home. If you ain't gone too long."

"Where's home, baby?"

The girl stared at him. A half-smile moved along her full lips, died at the corners of them. The breeze picked a sheet of newspaper out of the gutter and tossed it against the man's leg. He kicked at it savagely.

"Calliope Apartments. Four–B, Two-Forty-Six East Forty-Eight. How soon you be there?"

The man stepped very close to her, reached back and tapped his hip. His voice was low, chilling.

"You wait for me, baby."

She caught her breath, nodded. "Okey, handsome. I'll wait."

The man went back along the cracked sidewalk, across the intersection, along to where the stencil sign hung out over the street. He went through a glass door into a narrow lobby with a row of brown wooden chairs pushed against the plaster wall. There was just space to walk past them to the desk. A bald-headed colored man lounged behind the desk, fingering a large green pin in his tie.

The Negro in the purple suit leaned across the counter and his teeth flashed in a quick, hard smile. He was very young, with a thin, sharp jaw, a narrow bony forehead, the flat brilliant eyes of the gangster. He said softly: "That pug with the husky voice still here? The guy that banked the crap game last night."

The bald-headed clerk looked at the flies on the ceiling fixture. "Didn't see him go out, Smiler."

"Ain't what I asked you, Doc."

"Yeah. He still here."

"Still drunk?"

"Guess so. Hasn't been out."

"Three-forty-nine, ain't it?"

"You been there, ain't you? What you wanta know for?"

"He cleaned me down to my lucky piece. I gotta make a touch."

The bald-headed man looked nervous. The Smiler stared softly at the green stone in the man's tie pin.

"Get rolling, Smiler. Nobody gets bent around here. We ain't no Central Avenue flop."

The Smiler said very softly: "He's my pal, Doc. He'll lend me twenty. You touch half."

He put his hand out palm up. The clerk stared at the hand for a long moment. Then he nodded sourly, went behind a ground-glass screen, came back slowly, looking toward the street door.

His hand went out and hovered over the palm. The palm closed over a passkey, dropped inside the cheap purple suit.

The sudden flashing grin on the Smiler's face had an icy edge to it.

"Careful, Doc—while I'm up above."

The clerk said: "Step on it. Some of the customers get home early." He glanced at the green electric clock on the wall. It was seven-fifteen. "And the walls ain't any too thick," he added.

The thin youth gave him another flashing grin, nodded, went delicately back along the lobby to the shadowy staircase. There was no elevator in the Surprise Hotel.

At one minute past seven Pete Anglich, narcotic squad under-cover man, rolled over on the hard bed and looked at the cheap strap watch on his left wrist. There were heavy shadows under his eyes, a thick dark stubble on his broad chin. He swung his bare feet to the floor and stood up in cheap cotton pajamas, flexed his muscles, stretched, bent over stiff-kneed and touched the floor in front of his toes with a grunt.

He walked across to a chipped bureau, drank from a quart bottle of cheap rye whiskey, grimaced, pushed the cork into the neck of the bottle, and rammed it down hard with the heel of his hand.

"Boy, have I got a hangover," he grumbled huskily.

He stared at his face in the bureau mirror, at the stubble on his chin, the thick white scar on his throat close to the windpipe. His voice was husky because the bullet that had made the scar had done something to his vocal chords. It was a smooth huskiness, like the voice of a blues singer.

He stripped his pajamas off and stood naked in the middle of the room, his toes fumbling the rough edge of a big rip in the carpet. His body was very broad, and that made him look a little shorter than he was. His shoulders sloped, his nose was a little thick, the skin over his cheekbones looked like leather. He had short, curly, black hair, utterly steady eyes, the small set mouth of a quick thinker.

He went into a dim, dirty bathroom, stepped into the tub and turned the shower on. The water was warmish, but not hot. He stood under it and soaped himself, rubbed his whole body over, kneaded his muscles, rinsed off.

He jerked a dirty towel off the rack and started to rub a glow into his skin.

A faint noise behind the loosely closed bathroom door stopped him. He held his breath, listened, heard the noise again, a creak of boarding, a click, a rustle of cloth. Pete Anglich reached for the door and pulled it open slowly.

The Negro in the purple suit and Panama hat stood beside the bureau, with Pete Anglich's coat in his hand. On the bureau in front of him were two guns. One of them was Pete Anglich's old worn Colt. The room door was shut and a key with a tag lay on the carpet near it, as though it had fallen out of the door, or been pushed out from the other side.

The Smiler let the coat fall to the floor and held a wallet in his left hand. His right hand lifted the Colt. He grinned.

"Okey, white boy. Just go on dryin' yourself off after your shower," he said.

Pete Anglich toweled himself. He rubbed himself dry, stood naked with the wet towel in his left hand.

The Smiler had the billfold empty on the bureau, was counting the money with his left hand. His right still clutched the Colt.

"Eighty-seven bucks. Nice money. Some of it's mine from the crap game, but I'm lifting it all, pal. Take it easy. I'm friends with the management here."

"Gimme a break, Smiler," Pete Anglich said hoarsely. "That's every dollar I got in the world. Leave a few bucks, huh?" He made his voice thick, coarse, heavy as though with liquor.

The Smiler gleamed his teeth, shook his narrow head. "Can't do it, pal. Got me a date and I need the kale."

Pete Anglich took a loose step forward and stopped, grinning sheepishly. The muzzle of his own gun had jerked at him.

The Smiler sidled over to the bottle of rye and lifted it.

"I can use this, too. My baby's got a throat for liquor. Sure has. What's in your pants is yours, pal. Fair enough?"

Pete Anglich jumped sideways, about four feet. The

Smiler's face convulsed. The gun jerked around and the bottle of rye slid out of his left hand, slammed down on his foot. He yelped, kicked out savagely, and his toe caught in the torn place in the carpet.

Pete Anglich flipped the wet end of the bathtowel straight at the Smiler's eyes.

The Smiler reeled and yelled with pain. Then Pete Anglich held the Smiler's gun wrist in his hard left hand. He twisted up, around. His hand started to slide down over the Smiler's hand, over the gun. The gun turned inward and touched the Smiler's side.

A hard knee kicked viciously at Pete Anglich's abdomen. He gagged, and his finger tightened convulsively on the Smiler's trigger finger.

The shot was dull, muffled against the purple cloth of the suit. The Smiler's eyes rolled whitely and his narrow jaw fell slack.

Pete Anglich let him down on the floor and stood panting, bent over, his face greenish. He groped for the fallen bottle of rye, got the cork out, got some of the fiery liquid down his throat.

The greenish look went away from his face. His breathing slowed. He wiped sweat off his forehead with the back of his hand.

He felt the Smiler's pulse. The Smiler didn't have any pulse. He was dead. Pete Anglich loosened the gun from his hand, went over to the door and glanced out into the hallway. Empty. There was a passkey in the outside of the lock. He removed it, locked the door from the inside.

He put his underclothes and socks and shoes on, his worn blue serge suit, knotted a black tie around the crumpled shirt collar, went back to the dead man and took a roll of bills from his pocket. He packed a few odds and ends of clothes and toilet articles in a cheap fiber suitcase, stood it by the door.

He pushed a torn scrap of sheet through his revolver barrel with a pencil, replaced the used cartridge, crushed the empty shell with his heel on the bathroom floor and then flushed it down the toilet.

He locked the door from the outside and walked down the stairs to the lobby.

The bald-headed clerk's eyes jumped at him, then dropped. The skin of his face turned gray. Pete Anglich leaned on the counter and opened his hand to let two keys tinkle on the scarred wood. The clerk stared at the keys, shuddered.

Pete Anglich said in his slow, husky voice: "Hear any funny noises?"

The clerk shook his head, gulped.

"Creep joint, eh?" Pete Anglich said.

The clerk moved his head painfully, twisted his neck in his collar. His bald head winked darkly under the ceiling light.

"Too bad," Pete Anglich said. "What name did I register under last night?"

"You ain't registered," the clerk whispered.

"Maybe I wasn't here even," Pete Anglich said softly.

"Never saw you before, mister."

"You're not seeing me now. You never will see me—to know me—will you, Doc?"

The clerk moved his neck and tried to smile.

Pete Anglich drew his wallet out and shook three dollar bills from it.

"I'm a guy that likes to pay his way," he said slowly. "This pays for Room 349—till way in the morning, kind of late. The lad you gave the passkey to looks like a heavy sleeper." He paused, steadied his cool eyes on the clerk's face, added thoughtfully: "Unless, of course, he's got friends who would like to move him out."

Bubbles showed on the clerk's lips. He stuttered: "He ain't—ain't—"

"Yeah," Pete Anglich said. "What would you expect?"

He went across to the street door, carrying his

suitcase, stepped out under the stencil sign, stood a moment looking toward the hard white glare of Central Avenue.

Then he walked the other way. The street was very dark, very quiet. There were four blocks of frame houses before he came to Noon Street. It was all a Negro quarter.

He met only one person on the way, a brown girl in a green hat, very sheer stockings, and four-and-a-half-inch heels, who smoked a cigarette under a dusty palm tree and stared back toward the Surprise Hotel.

## 2

The lunch wagon was an old buffet car without wheels, set end to the street in a space between a machine shop and a rooming house. The name Bella Donna was lettered in faded gold on the sides. Pete Anglich went up the two iron steps at the end, into a smell of fry grease.

The Negro cook's fat white back was to him. At the far end of the low counter a white girl in a cheap brown felt hat and a shabby polo coat with a high turned-up collar was sipping coffee, her cheek propped in her left hand. There was nobody else in the car.

Pete Anglich put his suitcase down and sat on a stool near the door, saying: "Hi, Mopsy!"

The fat cook turned a shiny black face over his white shoulder. The face split in a grin. A thick bluish tongue came out and wiggled between the cook's thick lips.

"How's a boy? W'at you eat?"

"Scramble two light, coffee, toast, no spuds."

"Dat ain't no food for a he-guy," Mopsy complained.

"I been drunk," Pete Anglich said.

The girl at the end of the counter looked at him sharply, looked at the cheap alarm clock on the shelf,

at the watch on her gloved wrist. She drooped, stared
into her coffee cup again.

The fat cook broke eggs into a pan, added milk,
stirred them around. "You want a shot, boy?"

Pete Anglich shook his head.

"I'm driving the wagon, Mopsy."

The cook grinned. He reached a brown bottle from
under the counter, and poured a big drink into a water
glass, set the glass down beside Pete Anglich.

Pete Anglich reached suddenly for the glass, jerked it
to his lips, drank the liquor down.

"Guess I'll drive the wagon some other time." He
put the glass down empty.

The girl stood up, came along the stools, put a dime
on the counter. The fat cook punched his cash register,
put down a nickel change. Pete Anglich stared casually
at the girl. A shabby, innocent-eyed girl, brown hair
curling on her neck, eyebrows plucked clean as a bone
and startled arches painted above the place where they
had been.

"Not lost, are you, lady?" he asked in his softly
husky voice.

The girl had fumbled her bag open to put the nickel
away. She started violently, stepped back and dropped
the bag. It spilled its contents on the floor. She stared
down at it, wide-eyed.

Pete Anglich went down on one knee and pushed
things into the bag. A cheap nickel compact, cigarettes,
a purple matchfolder lettered in gold: The Juggernaut
Club. Two colored handkerchiefs, a crumpled dollar
bill and some silver and pennies.

He stood up with the closed bag in his hand, held it
out to the girl.

"Sorry," he said softly. "I guess I startled you."

Her breath made a rushing sound. She caught the
bag out of his hand, ran out of the car, and was gone.

The fat cook looked after her. "That doll don't belong in Tough Town," he said slowly.

He dished up the eggs and toast, poured coffee in a thick cup, put them down in front of Pete Anglich.

Pete Anglich touched the food, said absently: "Alone, and matches from the Juggernaut. Trimmer Waltz's spot. You know what happens to girls like that when he gets hold of them."

The cook licked his lips, reached under the counter for the whiskey bottle. He poured himself a drink, added about the same amount of water to the bottle, put it back under the counter.

"I ain't never been a tough guy, and don' want to start," he said slowly. "But I'se all tired of white boys like dat guy. Some day he gonna get cut."

Pete Anglich kicked his suitcase.

"Yeah. Keep the keister for me, Mopsy."

He went out.

Two or three cars flicked by in the crisp fall night, but the sidewalks were dark and empty. A colored night watchman moved slowly along the street, trying the doors of a small row of dingy stores. There were frame houses across the street, and a couple of them were noisy.

Pete Anglich went on past the intersection. Three blocks from the lunch wagon he saw the girl again.

She was pressed against a wall, motionless. A little beyond her, dim yellow light came from the stairway of a walk-up apartment house. Beyond that a small parking lot with billboards across most of its front. Faint light from somewhere touched her hat, her shabby polo coat with the turned-up collar, one side of her face. He knew it was the same girl.

He stepped into a doorway, watched her. Light flashed on her upraised arm, on something bright, a wrist watch. Somewhere not far off a clock struck eight, low, pealing notes.

Lights stabbed into the street from the corner behind. A big car swung slowly into view and as it swung its headlights dimmed. It crept along the block, a dark shininess of glass and polished paint.

Pete Anglich grinned sharply in his doorway. A custom-built Duesenberg, six blocks from Central Avenue! He stiffened at the sharp sound of running steps, clicking high heels.

The girl was running toward him along the sidewalk. The car was not near enough for its dimmed lights to pick her up. Pete Anglich stepped out of the doorway, grabbed her arm, dragged her back into the doorway. A gun snaked from under his coat.

The girl panted at his side.

The Duesenberg passed the doorway slowly. No shots came from it. The uniformed driver didn't slow down.

"I can't do it. I'm scared," the girl gasped in Pete Anglich's ear. Then she broke away from him and ran farther along the sidewalk, away from the car.

Pete Anglich looked after the Duesenberg. It was opposite the row of billboards that screened the parking lot. It was barely crawling now. Something sailed from its left front window, fell with a dry slap on the sidewalk. The car picked up speed soundlessly, purred off into the darkness. A block away its head lights flashed up full again.

Nothing moved. The thing that had been thrown out of the car lay on the inner edge of the sidewalk, almost under one of the billboards.

Then the girl was coming back again, a step at a time, haltingly. Pete Anglich watched her come, without moving. When she was level with him he said softly: "What's the racket? Could a fellow help?"

She spun around with a choked sound, as though she had forgotten all about him. Her head moved in the darkness at his side. There was a swift shine as her eyes moved. There was a pale flicker across her chin. Her voice was low, hurried, scared.

"You're the man from the lunch wagon. I saw you."

"Open up. What is it—a pay-off?"

Her head moved again in the darkness at his side, up and down.

"What's in the package?" Pete Anglich growled. "Money?"

Her words came in a rush. "Would you get it for me? Oh, would you please? I'd be so grateful. I'd—"

He laughed. His laugh had a low growling sound. "Get it for *you*, baby? I use money in my business, too. Come on, what's the racket? Spill."

She jerked away from him, but he didn't let go of her arm. He slid the gun out of sight under his coat, held her with both hands. Her voice sobbed as she whispered: "He'll kill me, if I don't get it."

Very sharply, coldly, Pete Anglich said, "Who will? Trimmer Waltz?"

She started violently, almost tore out of his grasp. Not quite. Steps shuffled on the sidewalk. Two dark forms showed in front of the billboards, didn't pause to pick anything up. The steps came near, cigarette tips glowed.

A voice said softly: " 'Lo there, sweets. Yo' want to change yo'r boy frien', honey?"

The girl shrank behind Pete Anglich. One of the Negroes laughed gently, waved the red end of his cigarette.

"Hell, it's a white gal," the other one said quickly. "Le's dust."

They went on, chuckling. At the corner they turned, were gone.

"There you are," Pete Anglich growled. "Shows you where you are." His voice was hard, angry. "Oh, hell, stay here and I'll get your damn pay-off for you."

He left the girl and went lightly along close to the front of the apartment house. At the edge of the billboards he stopped, probed the darkness with his eyes, saw the package. It was wrapped in dark material, not large but large enough to see. He bent down and looked under the billboards. He didn't see anything behind them.

He went on four steps, leaned down and picked up the package, felt cloth and two thick rubber bands. He stood quite still, listening.

Distant traffic hummed on a main street. A light burned across the street in a rooming house, behind a glass-paneled door. A window was open and dark above it.

A woman's voice screamed shrilly behind him.

He stiffened, whirled, and the light hit him between the eyes. It came from the dark window across the street, a blinding white shaft that impaled him against the billboard.

His face leered in it, his eyes blinked. He didn't move any more.

Shoes dropped on cement and a smaller spot stabbed at him sideways from the end of the billboards. Behind the spot a casual voice spoke: "Don't shift an eyelash, bud. You're all wrapped up in law."

Men with revolvers out closed in on him from both ends of the line of billboards. Heels clicked far off on concrete. Then it was silent for a moment. Then a car with a red spotlight swung around the corner and bore down on the group of men with Pete Anglich in their midst.

The man with the casual voice said: "I'm Angus, detective-lieutenant. I'll take the packet, if you don't mind. And if you'll just keep your hands together a minute—"

The handcuffs clicked dryly on Pete Anglich's wrists.

He listened hard for the sound of the heels far off, running away. But there was too much noise around him now.

Doors opened and dark people began to boil out of the houses.

## 3

John Vidaury was six feet two inches in height and had the most perfect profile in Hollywood. He was dark, winsome, romantic, with an interesting touch of gray at his temples. His shoulders were wide, his hips narrow. He had the waist of an English guards officer, and his dinner clothes fit him so beautifully that it hurt.

So he looked at Pete Anglich as if he was about to apologize for not knowing him. Pete Anglich looked at his handcuffs, at his worn shoes on the thick rug, at the tall chiming clock against the wall. There was a flush on his face and his eyes were bright.

In a smooth, clear, modulated voice Vidaury said, "No, I've never seen him before." He smiled at Pete Anglich.

Angus, the plainclothes lieutenant, leaned against one end of a carved library table and snapped a finger against the brim of his hat. Two other detectives stood near a side wall. A fourth sat at a small desk with a stenographer's notebook in front of him.

Angus said, "Oh, we just thought you might know him. We can't get much of anything out of him."

Vidaury raised his eyebrows, smiled very faintly. "Really I'm surprised at that." He went around collecting glasses, and took them over to a tray, started to mix more drinks.

"It happens," Angus said.

"I thought you had ways," Vidaury said delicately, pouring Scotch into the glasses.

Angus looked at a fingernail. "When I say he won't tell us anything, Mr. Vidaury, I mean anything that counts. He says his name is Pete Anglich, that he used to be a fighter, but hasn't fought for several years. Up to about a year ago he was a private detective, but has no work now. He won some money in a crap game and got drunk, and was just wandering about. That's how he happened to be on Noon Street. He saw the package tossed out of your car and picked it up. We can vag him, but that's about all."

"It could happen that way," Vidaury said softly. He carried the glasses two at a time to the four detectives, lifted his own, and nodded slightly before he drank. He drank gracefully, with a superb elegance of movement. "No, I don't know him," he said again. "Frankly, he doesn't look like an acid-thrower to me." He waved a hand. "So I'm afraid bringing him here—"

Pete Anglich lifted his head suddenly, stared at Vidaury. His voice sneered.

"It's a great compliment, Vidaury. They don't often use up the time of four coppers taking prisoners around to call on people."

Vidaury smiled amiably. "That's Hollywood," he smiled. "After all, one had a reputation."

"Had," Pete Anglich said. "Your last picture was a pain where you don't tell the ladies."

Angus stiffened. Vidaury's face went white. He put his glass down slowly, let his hand fall to his side. He walked springily across the rug and stood in front of Pete Anglich.

"That's your opinion," he said harshly, "but I warn you——"

Pete Anglich scowled at him. "Listen, big shot. You put a grand on the line because some punk promised to throw acid at you if you didn't. I picked up the grand, but I didn't get any of your nice, new money. So you got it back. You get ten grand worth of publicity and it won't cost you a nickel. I call that pretty swell."

Angus said sharply, "That's enough from you, mug."

"Yeah?" Pete Anglich sneered. "I thought you wanted me to talk. Well, I'm talking, and I hate pikers, see?"

Vidaury breathed hard. Very suddenly he balled his fist and swung at Pete Anglich's jaw. Pete Anglich's head rolled under the blow, and his eyes blinked shut, then wide open. He shook himself and said coolly:

"Elbow up and thumb down, Vidaury. You break a hand hitting a guy that way."

Vidaury stepped back and shook his head, looked at his thumb. His face lost its whiteness. His smile stole back.

"I'm sorry," he said contritely. "I am very sorry. I'm not used to being insulted. As I don't know this man, perhaps you'd better take him away, Lieutenant. Handcuffed, too. Not very sporting, was it?"

"Tell that to your polo ponies," Pete Anglich said. "I don't bruise so easy."

Angus walked over to him, tapped his shoulder. "Up on the dogs, bo. Let's drift. You're not used to nice people, are you?"

"No. I like bums," Pete Anglich said.

He stood up slowly, scuffed at the pile of the carpet.

The two dicks against the wall fell in beside him, and they walked away down the huge room, under an arch. Angus and the other man came behind. They waited in the small private lobby for the elevator to come up.

"What was the idea?" Angus snapped. "Getting gashouse with him?"

Pete Anglich laughed. "Jumpy," he said. "Just jumpy."

The elevator came up and they rode down to the huge, silent lobby of the Chester Towers. Two house detectives lounged at the end of the marble desk, two clerks stood alert behind it.

Pete Anglich lifted his manacled hands in the fighter's salute. "What, no newshawks yet?" he jeered. "Vidaury won't like hush-hush on this."

"Keep goin', smartie," one of the dicks snapped, jerking his arm.

They went down a corridor and out of a side entrance to a narrow street that dropped almost sheer to treetops. Beyond the treetops the lights of the city were a vast golden carpet, stitched with brilliant splashes of red and green and blue and purple.

Two starters whirred. Pete Anglich was pushed into the back seat of the first car. Angus and another man got in on either side of him. The cars drifted down the hill, turned east on Fountain, slid quietly through the evening for mile after mile. Fountain met Sunset, and the cars dropped downtown toward the tall, white tower of the City Hall. At the plaza the first car swung over to Los Angeles Street and went south. The other car went on.

After a while Pete Anglich dropped the corners of his mouth and looked sideways at Angus.

"Where you taking me? This isn't the way to headquarters."

Angus' dark, austere face turned toward him slowly. After a moment the big detective leaned back and yawned at the night. He didn't answer.

The car slid along Los Angeles to Fifth, east to San Pedro, south again for block after block, quiet blocks and loud blocks, blocks where silent men sat on shaky front porches and blocks where noisy young toughs of both colors snarled and wisecracked at one another in front of cheap restaurants and drugstores and beer parlors full of slot machines.

At Santa Barbara the police car turned east again, drifted slowly along the curb to Noon Street. It stopped at the corner above the lunch wagon. Pete Anglich's face tightened again, but he didn't say anything.

"Okey," Angus drawled. "Take the nippers off."

The dick on Pete Anglich's other side dug a key out of his vest, unlocked the handcuffs, jangled them pleasantly before he put them away on his hip. Angus swung the door open and stepped out of the car.

"Out," he said over his shoulder.

Pete Anglich got out. Angus walked a little way from the street light, stopped, beckoned. His hand moved under his coat, came out with a gun. He said softly: "Had to play it this way. Otherwise we'd tip the town. Pearson's the only one that knows you. Any ideas?"

Pete Anglich took his gun, shook his head slowly, slid the gun under his own coat, keeping his body between it and the car at the curb behind.

"The stake-out was spotted, I guess," he said slowly. "There was a girl hanging around there, but maybe that just happened, too."

Angus stared at him silently for a moment, then nodded and went back to the car. The door slammed shut, and the car drifted off down the street and picked up speed.

Pete Anglich walked along Santa Barbara to Central, south on Central. After a while a bright sign glared at him in violet letters—Juggernaut Club. He went up broad carpeted stairs toward noise and dance music.

### 4

The girl had to go sideways to get between the close-set tables around the small dance floor. Her hips touched the back of a man's shoulder and he reached out and grabbed her hand, grinning. She smiled mechanically, pulled her hand away and came on.

She looked better in the bronze metal-cloth dress with bare arms and the brown hair curling low on her neck; better than in the shabby polo coat and cheap felt hat, better even than in skyscraper heels, bare legs and thighs, the irreducible minimum above the waistline, and a dull gold opera hat tipped rakishly over one ear.

Her face looked haggard, small, pretty, shallow. Her eyes had a wide stare. The dance band made a sharp racket over the clatter of dishes, the thick hum of talk, the shuffling feet on the dance floor. The girl came slowly up to Pete Anglich's table, pulled the other chair out and sat down.

She propped her chin on the backs of her hands, put her elbows on the tablecloth, stared at him.

"Hello there," she said in a voice that shook a little.

Pete Anglich pushed a pack of cigarettes across the table, watched her shake one loose and get it between her lips. He struck a match. She had to take it out of his hand to light her cigarette.

"Drink?"

"I'll say."

He signaled the fuzzy-haired, almond-eyed waiter, ordered a couple of sidecars. The waiter went away. Pete Anglich leaned back on his chair and looked at one of his blunt fingertips.

The girl said very softly: "I got your note, mister."

"Like it?" His voice was stiffly casual. He didn't look at her.

She laughed off key. "We've got to please the customers."

Pete Anglich looked past her shoulder at the corner of the band shell. A man stood there smoking, beside a small microphone. He was heavily built, old for an m.c., with slick gray hair and a big nose and the thickened complexion of a steady drinker. He was smiling at everything and everybody. Pete Anglich looked at him a little while, watching the direction of his glances. He said stiffly, in the same casual voice, "But you'd be here anyway."

The girl stiffened, then slumped. "You don't have to insult me, mister."

He looked at her slowly, with an empty up-from-under look. "You're down and out, knee-deep in nothing, baby. I've been that way often enough to know the symptoms. Besides, you got me in plenty jam tonight. I owe you a couple insults."

The fuzzy-haired waiter came back and slid a tray on the cloth, wiped the bottoms of two glasses with a dirty towel, set them out. He went away again.

The girl put her hand around a glass, lifted it quickly and took a long drink. She shivered a little as she put the glass down. Her face was white.

"Wisecrack or something," she said rapidly. "Don't just sit there. I'm watched."

Pete Anglich touched his fresh drink, smiled very deliberately toward the corner of the band shell.

"Yeah, I can imagine. Tell me about that pick-up on Noon Street."

She reached out quickly and touched his arm. Her sharp nails dug into it. "Not here," she breathed. "I don't know how you found me and I don't care. You looked like the kind of Joe that would help a girl out. I was scared stiff. But don't talk about it here. I'll do anything you want, go anywhere you want. Only not here."

Pete Anglich took his arm from under her hand, leaned back again. His eyes were cold, but his mouth was kind.

"I get it. Trimmer's wishes. Was he tailing the job?"

She nodded quickly. "I hadn't gone three blocks before he picked me up. He thought it was a swell gag, what I did, but he won't think so when he sees you here. That makes you wise."

Pete Anglich sipped his drink. "He is coming this way," he said, coolly.

The gray-haired m.c. was moving among the tables, bowing and talking, but edging toward the one where Pete Anglich sat with the girl. The girl was staring into a big gilt mirror behind Pete Anglich's head. Her face was suddenly distorted, shattered with terror. Her lips were shaking uncontrollably.

Trimmer Waltz idled casually up to the table, leaned a hand down on it. He poked his big-veined nose at Pete Anglich. There was a soft, flat grin on his face.

"Hi, Pete. Haven't seen you around since they buried McKinley. How's tricks?"

"Not bad, not good," Pete Anglich said huskily. "I been on a drunk."

Trimmer Waltz broadened his smile, turned it on the

girl. She looked at him quickly, looked away, picking at the tablecloth.

Waltz's voice was soft, cooing. "Know the little lady before—or just pick her out of the line-up?"

Pete Anglich shrugged, looked bored. "Just wanted somebody to share a drink with, Trimmer. Sent her a note. Okey?"

"Sure. Perfect." Waltz picked one of the glasses up, sniffed at it. He shook his head sadly. "Wish we could serve better stuff. At four bits a throw it can't be done. How about tipping a few out of a right bottle, back in my den?"

"Both of us?" Pete Anglich asked gently.

"Both of you is right. In about five minutes. I got to circulate a little first."

He pinched the girl's cheek, went on, with a loose swing of his tailored shoulders.

The girl said slowly, thickly, hopelessly, "So Pete's your name. You must want to die young, Pete. Mine's Token Ware. Silly name, isn't it?"

"I like it," Pete Anglich said softly.

The girl stared at a point below the white scar on Pete Anglich's throat. Her eyes slowly filled with tears.

Trimmer Waltz drifted among the tables, speaking to a customer here and there. He edged over to the far wall, came along it to the band shell, stood there ranging the house with his eyes until he was looking directly at Pete Anglich. He jerked his head, stepped back through a pair of thick curtains.

Pete Anglich pushed his chair back and stood up. "Let's go," he said.

Token Ware crushed a cigarette out in a glass tray with jerky fingers, finished the drink in her glass, stood up. They went back between the tables, along the edge of the dance floor, over to the side of the band shell.

The curtains opened on to a dim hallway with doors on both sides. A shabby red carpet masked the floor. The walls were chipped, the doors cracked.

"The one at the end on the left," Token Ware whispered.

They came to it. Pete Anglich knocked. Trimmer Waltz's voice called out to come in. Pete Anglich stood a moment looking at the door, then turned his head and looked at the girl with his eyes hard and narrow. He pushed the door open, gestured at her. They went in.

The room was not very light. A small oblong reading lamp on the desk shed glow on polished wood, but less on the shabby red carpet, and the long heavy red drapes across the outer wall. The air was close, with a thick, sweetish smell of liquor.

Trimmer Waltz sat behind the desk with his hands touching a tray that contained a cut-glass decanter, some gold-veined glasses, an ice bucket and a siphon of charged water.

He smiled, rubbed one side of his big nose.

"Park yourselves, folks. Liqueur Scotch at six-ninety a fifth. That's what it costs me—wholesale."

Pete Anglich shut the door, looked slowly around the room, at the floor-length window drapes, at the unlighted ceiling light. He unbuttoned the top button of his coat with a slow, easy movement.

"Hot in here," he said softly. "Any windows behind those drapes?"

The girl sat in a round chair on the opposite side of the desk from Waltz. He smiled at her very gently.

"Good idea," Waltz said. "Open one up, will you?"

Pete Anglich went past the end of the desk, toward the curtains. As he got beyond Waltz, his hand went up under his coat and touched the butt of his gun. He moved softly toward the red drapes. The tips of wide, square-toed black shoes just barely showed under the curtains, in the shadow between the curtains and the wall.

Pete Anglich reached the curtains, put his left hand out and jerked them open.

The shoes on the floor against the wall were empty.

Waltz laughed dryly behind Pete Anglich. Then a thick, cold voice said: "Put 'em high, boy."

The girl made a strangled sound, not quite a scream. Pete Anglich dropped his hands and turned slowly and looked. The Negro was enormous in stature, gorilla-like, and wore a baggy checked suit that made him even more enormous. He had come soundlessly on shoeless feet out of a closet door, and his right hand almost covered a huge black gun.

Trimmer Waltz held a gun too, a Savage. The two men stared quietly at Pete Anglich. Pete Anglich put his hands up in the air, his eyes blank, his small mouth set hard.

The Negro in the checked suit came toward him in long, loose strides, pressed the gun against his chest, then reached under his coat. His hand came out with Pete Anglich's gun. He dropped it behind him on the floor. He shifted his own gun casually and hit Pete Anglich on the side of the jaw with the flat of it.

Pete Anglich staggered and the salt taste of blood came under his tongue. He blinked, said thickly: "I'll remember you a long time, big boy."

The Negro grinned. "Not so long, pal. Not so long."

He hit Pete Anglich again with the gun, then suddenly he jammed it into a side pocket and his two big hands shot out, clamped themselves on Pete Anglich's throat.

"When they's tough I likes to squeeze 'em," he said almost softly.

Thumbs that felt as big and hard as doorknobs pressed into the arteries on Pete Anglich's neck. The face before him and above him grew enormous, an enormous shadowy face with a wide grin in the middle of it. It waved in lessening light, an unreal, a fantastic face.

Pete Anglich hit the face, with puny blows, the blows of a toy balloon. His fists didn't feel anything as they hit the face. The big man twisted him around and put a knee into his back, and bent him down over the knee.

There was no sound for a while except the thunder of blood threshing in Pete Anglich's head. Then, far away, he seemed to hear a girl scream thinly. From still farther away the voice of Trimmer Waltz muttered: "Easy now, Rufe. Easy."

A vast blackness shot with hot red filled Pete Anglich's world. The darkness grew silent. Nothing moved in it now, not even blood.

The Negro lowered Pete Anglich's limp body to the floor, stepped back and rubbed his hands together.

"Yeah, I likes to squeeze 'em," he said.

## 5

The Negro in the checked suit sat on the side of the daybed and picked languidly at a five-stringed banjo. His large face was solemn and peaceful, a little sad. He plucked the banjo strings slowly, with his bare fingers, his head on one side, a crumpled cigarette-end sticking barely past his lips at one corner of his mouth.

Low down in his throat he was making a kind of droning sound. He was singing.

A cheap electric clock on the mantel said 11.35. It was a small living room with bright, overstuffed furniture, a red floor lamp with a cluster of French dolls at its base, a gay carpet with large diamond shapes in it, two curtained windows with a mirror between them.

A door at the back was ajar. A door near it opening into the hall was shut.

Pete Anglich lay on his back on the floor, with his mouth open and his arms outflung. His breath was a thick snore. His eyes were shut, and his face in the reddish glow of the lamp looked flushed and feverish.

The Negro put the banjo down out of his immense hands, stood up and yawned and stretched. He walked across the room and looked at a calendar over the mantel.

"This ain't August," he said disgustedly.

He tore a leaf from the calendar, rolled it into a ball and threw it at Pete Anglich's face. It hit the unconscious man's cheek. He didn't stir. The Negro spit the cigarette-end into his palm, held his palm out flat, and flicked a fingernail at it, sent it sailing in the same direction as the paper ball.

He loafed a few steps and leaned down, fingering a bruise on Pete Anglich's temple. He pressed the bruise, grinning softly. Pete Anglich didn't move.

The Negro straightened and kicked the unconscious man in the ribs thoughtfully, over and over again, not very hard. Pete Anglich moved a little, gurgled, and rolled his head to one side. The Negro looked pleased, left him, went back to the daybed. He carried his banjo over to the hall door and leaned it against the wall. There was a gun lying on a newspaper on a small table. He went through a partly open inner door and came back with a pint bottle of gin, half full. He rubbed the bottle over carefully with a handkerchief, set it on the mantel.

"About time now, pal," he mused out loud. "When you wake up, maybe you don't feel so good. Maybe need a shot . . . Hey, I gotta better hunch."

He reached for the bottle again, went down on one big knee, poured gin over Pete Anglich's mouth and chin, slopped it loosely on the front of his shirt. He stood the bottle on the floor, after wiping it off again, and flicked the glass stopper under the daybed.

"Grab it, white boy," he said softly. "Prints don't never hurt."

He got the newspaper with the gun on it, slid the gun off on the carpet, and moved it with his foot until it lay just out of reach of Pete Anglich's outflung hand.

He studied the layout carefully from the door,

nodded, picked his banjo up. He opened the door, peeped out, then looked back.

"So long, pal," he said softly. "Time for me to breeze. You ain't got a lot of future comin', but what you got you get sudden."

He shut the door, went along the hallway to stairs and down the stairs. Radios made faint sound behind shut doors. The entrance lobby of the apartment house was empty. The Negro in the checked suit slipped into a pay booth in the dark corner of the lobby, dropped his nickel and dialed.

A heavy voice said: "Police department."

The Negro put his lips close to the transmitter and got a whine into his voice.

"This the cops? Say, there's been a shootin' scrape in the Calliope Apartments, Two-Forty-Six East Forty-Eight, Apartment Four—B. Got it? . . . Well, do somethin' about it, flatfoot!"

He hung up quickly, giggling, ran down the front steps of the apartment house and jumped into a small, dirty sedan. He kicked it to life and drove toward Central Avenue. He was a block from Central Avenue when the red eye of a prowl car swung around from Central on to East Forty-Eight Street.

The Negro in the sedan chuckled and went on his way. He was singing down in his throat when the prowl car whirred past him.

The instant the door latch clicked Pete Anglich opened his eyes halfway. He turned his head slowly, and a grin of pain came on his face and stayed on it, but he kept on turning his head until he could see the emptiness of one end of the room and the middle. He tipped his head far back on the floor, saw the rest of the room.

He rolled toward the gun and took hold of it. It was his own gun. He sat up and snapped the gate open mechanically. His face stiffened out of the grin. One shell in the gun had been fired. The barrel smelled of powder fumes.

He came to his feet and crept toward the slightly open inner door, keeping his head low. When he reached the door he bent still lower, and slowly pushed the door wide open. Nothing happened. He looked into a bedroom with twin beds, made up and covered with rose damask with a gold design in it.

Somebody lay on one of the beds. A woman. She didn't move. The hard, tight grin came back on Pete Anglich's face. He rose straight up and walked softly on the balls of his feet over to the side of the bed. A door beyond was open on a bathroom, but no sound came from it. Pete Anglich looked down at the colored girl on the bed.

He caught his breath and let it out slowly. The girl was dead. Her eyes were half open, uninterested, her hands lazy at her sides. Her legs were twisted a little and bare skin showed above one sheer stocking, below the short skirt. A green hat lay on the floor. She had four-and-a-half-inch French heels. There was a scent of Midnight Narcissus in the room. He remembered the girl outside the Surprise Hotel.

She was quite dead, dead long enough for the blood to have clotted over the powder-scorched hole below her left breast.

Pete Anglich went back to the living room, grabbed up the gin bottle, and emptied it without stopping or choking. He stood a moment, breathing hard, thinking. The gun hung slack in his left hand. His small, tight mouth hardly showed at all.

He worked his fingers on the glass of the gin bottle, tossed it empty on top of the daybed, slid his gun into the underarm holster, went to the door and stepped quietly into the hall.

The hall was long and dim and yawning with chill air. A single bracket light loomed yellowly at the top of the stairs. A screen door led to a balcony over the front porch of the building. There was a gray splash of cold moonlight on one corner of the screen.

Pete Anglich went softly down the stairs to the front hall, put his hand out to the knob of the glass door.

A red spot hit the front of the door. It sifted a hard red glare through the glass and the sleazy curtain that masked it.

Pete Anglich slid down the door, below the panel, hunched along the wall to the side. His eyes ranged the place swiftly, held on the dark telephone booth.

"Man trap," he said softly, and dodged over to the booth, into it. He crouched and almost shut the door.

Steps slammed on the porch and the front door squeaked open. The steps hammered into the hallway, stopped.

A heavy voice said: "All quiet, huh? Maybe a phony."

Another voice said: "Four–B. Let's give it the dust, anyway."

The steps went along the lower hall, came back. They sounded on the stairs going up. They drummed in the upper hall.

Pete Anglich pushed the door of the booth back, slid over to the front door, crouched and squinted against the red glare.

The prowl car at the curb was a dark bulk. Its headlights burned along the cracked sidewalk. He couldn't see into it. He sighed, opened the door and walked quickly, but not too quickly, down the wooden steps from the porch.

The prowl car was empty, with both front doors hanging open. Shadowy forms were converging cautiously from across the street. Pete Anglich marched straight to the prowl car and got into it. He shut the doors quietly, stepped on the starter, threw the car in gear.

He drove off past the gathering crowd of neighbors. At the first corner he turned and switched off the red spot. Then he drove fast, wound in and out of blocks, away from Central, after a while turned back toward it.

When he was near its lights and chatter and traffic he pulled over to the side of the dusty tree-lined street, left the prowl car standing.

He walked towards Central.

## 6

Trimmer Waltz cradled the phone with his left hand. He put his right index finger along the edge of his upper lip, pushed the lip out of the way, and rubbed his finger slowly along his teeth and gums. His shallow, colorless eyes looked across the desk at the big Negro in the checked suit.

"Lovely," he said in a dead voice. "Lovely. He got away before the law jumped him. A very swell job, Rufe."

The Negro took a cigar stub out of his mouth and crushed it between a huge flat thumb and a huge flat forefinger.

"Hell, he was out cold," he snarled. "The prowlies passed me before I got to Central. Hell, he *can't* get away."

"That was him talking," Waltz said lifelessly. He opened the top drawer of his desk and laid his heavy Savage in front of him.

The Negro looked at the Savage. His eyes got dull and lightless, like obsidian. His lips puckered and gouged at each other.

"That gal's been cuttin' corners on me with three, four other guys," he grumbled. "I owed her the slug. Oky-doke. That's jake. Now, I go out and collect me the smart monkey."

He started to get up. Waltz barely touched the butt of his gun with two fingers. He shook his head, and the Negro sat down again. Waltz spoke.

"He got away, Rufe. And you called the buttons to find a dead woman. Unless they get him with the gun on him—one chance in a thousand—there's no way to tie it to him. That makes you the fall guy. You live there."

The Negro grinned and kept his dull eyes on the Savage.

He said: "That makes me get cold feet. And my feet are big enough to get plenty cold. Guess I take me a powder, huh?"

Waltz sighed. He said thoughtfully: "Yeah, I guess you leave town for a while. From Glendale. The 'Frisco late train will be about right."

The Negro looked sulky. "Nix on 'Frisco, boss. I put my thumbs on a frail there. She croaked. Nix on 'Frisco, boss."

"You've got ideas, Rufe," Waltz said calmly. He rubbed the side of his veined nose with one finger, then slicked his gray hair back with his palm. "I see them in your big brown eyes. Forget it. I'll take care of you. Get the car in the alley. We'll figure the angles on the way to Glendale."

The Negro blinked and wiped cigar ash off his chin with his huge hand.

"And better leave your big shiny gun here," Waltz added. "It needs a rest."

Rufe reached back and slowly drew his gun from a hip pocket. He pushed it across the polished wood of the desk with one finger. There was a faint, sleepy smile at the back of his eyes.

"Okey, boss," he said, almost dreamily.

He went across to the door, opened it, and went out. Waltz stood up and stepped over to the closet, put on a dark felt hat and a light-weight overcoat, a pair of dark gloves. He dropped the Savage into his left-hand pocket, Rufe's gun into the right. He went out of the room down the hall toward the sound of the dance band.

At the end he parted the curtains just enough to peer

through. The orchestra was playing a waltz. There was a good crowd, a quiet crowd for Central Avenue. Waltz sighed, watched the dancers for a moment, let the curtains fall together again.

He went back along the hall past his office to a door at the end that gave on stairs. Another door at the bottom of the stairs opened on a dark alley behind the building.

Waltz closed the door gently, stood in the darkness against the wall. The sound of an idling motor came to him, the light clatter of loose tappets. The alley was blind at one end, at the other turned at right angles toward the front of the building. Some of the light from Central Avenue splashed on a brick wall at the end of the cross alley, beyond the waiting car, a small sedan that looked battered and dirty even in the darkness.

Waltz reached his right hand into his overcoat pocket, took out Rufe's gun and held it down in the cloth of his overcoat. He waked to the sedan soundlessly, went around to the right-hand door, opened it to get in.

Two huge hands came out of the car and took hold of his throat. Hard hands, hands with enormous strength in them. Waltz made a faint gurgling sound before his head was bent back and his almost blind eyes were groping at the sky.

Then his right hand moved, moved like a hand that had nothing to do with his stiff, straining body, his tortured neck, his bulging blind eyes. It moved forward cautiously, delicately, until the muzzle of the gun it held pressed against something soft. It explored the something soft carefully, without haste, seemed to be making sure just what it was.

Trimmer Waltz didn't see, he hardly felt. He didn't breathe. But his hand obeyed his brain like a detached force beyond the reach of Rufe's terrible hands. Waltz's finger squeezed the trigger.

The hands fell slack on his throat, dropped away. He staggered back, almost fell across the alley, hit the far wall with his shoulder. He straightened slowly, gasping deep down in his tortured lungs. He began to shake.

He hardly noticed the big gorilla's body fall out of the car and slam the concrete at his feet. It lay at his feet, limp, enormous, but no longer menacing. No longer important.

Waltz dropped the gun on the sprawled body. He rubbed his throat gently for a little while. His breathing was deep, racking, noisy. He searched the inside of his mouth with his tongue, tasted blood. His eyes looked up wearily at the indigo slit of the night sky above the alley.

After a while he said huskily, "I thought of that, Rufe . . . You see, I thought of that."

He laughed, shuddered, adjusted his coat collar, went around the sprawled body to the car and reached in to switch the motor off. He started back along the alley to the rear door of the Juggernaut Club.

A man stepped out of the shadows at the back of the car. Waltz's left hand flashed to his overcoat pocket. Shiny metal blinked at him. He let his hand fall loosely at his side.

Pete Anglich said, "Thought that call would bring you out, Trimmer. Thought you might come this way. Nice going."

After a moment Waltz said thickly : "He choked me. It was self-defense."

"Sure. There's two of us with sore necks. Mine's a pip."

"What do you want, Pete?"

"You tried to frame me for bumping off a girl."

Waltz laughed suddenly, almost crazily. He said quietly: "When I'm crowded I get nasty, Pete. You should know that. Better lay off little Token Ware."

Pete Anglich moved his gun so that the light flickered on the barrel. He came up to Waltz, pushed the gun against his stomach.

"Rufe's dead," he said softly. "Very convenient. Where's the girl?"

"What's it to you?"

"Don't be a bunny. I'm wise. You tried to pick some jack off John Vidaury. I stepped in front of Token. I want to know the rest of it."

Waltz stood very still with the gun pressing his stomach. His fingers twisted in the gloves.

"Okay," he said dully. "How much to button your lip—and keep it buttoned?"

"Couple of centuries. Rufe lifted my poke."

"What does it buy me?" Waltz asked slowly.

"Not a damn thing. I want the girl, too."

Waltz said very gently: "Five C's. But not the girl. Five C's is heavy dough for a Central Avenue punk. Be smart and take it, and forget the rest."

The gun went away from his stomach. Pete Anglich circled him deftly, patted pockets, took the Savage, made a gesture with his left hand, holding it.

"Sold," he said grudgingly. "What's a girl between pals? Feed it to me."

"Have to go up to the office," Waltz said.

Pete Anglich laughed shortly. "Better play ball, Trimmer. Lead on."

They went back along the upstairs hall. The dance band beyond the distant curtains was wailing a Duke Ellington lament, a forlorn monotone of stifled brasses, bitter violins, softly clicking gourds. Waltz opened his office door, snapped the light on, went across to his desk and sat down. He tilted his hat back, smiled, opened a drawer with a key.

Pete Anglich watched him, reached back to turn the key in the door, went along the wall to the closet and looked into it, went behind Waltz to the curtains that masked the windows. He still had his gun out.

He came back to the end of the desk. Waltz was pushing a loose sheaf of bills away from him.

Pete Anglich ignored the money, leaned down over the end of the desk.

"Keep that and give me the girl, Trimmer."

Waltz shook his head, kept on smiling.

"The Vidaury squeeze was a grand, Trimmer—or started with a grand. Noon Street is almost in your alley. Do you have to scare women into doing your dirty work? I think you wanted something on the girl, so you could make her say uncle."

Waltz narrowed his eyes a little, pointed to the sheaf of bills.

Pete Anglich said slowly: "A shabby, lonesome, scared kid. Probably lives in a cheap furnished room. No friends, or she wouldn't be working in your joint. Nobody would wonder about her, except me. You wouldn't have put her in a house, would you, Trimmer?"

"Take your money and beat it," Waltz said thinly. "You know what happens to rats in this district."

"Sure, they run night clubs," Pete Anglich said gently.

He put his gun down, started to reach for the money. His fist doubled, swept upward casually. His elbow went up with the punch, the fist turned, landed almost delicately on the angle of Waltz's jaw.

Waltz became a loose bag of clothes. His mouth fell open. His hat fell off the back of his head. Pete Anglich stared at him, grumbled: "Lot of good that does me."

The room was very still. The dance band sounded faintly, like a turned-down radio. Pete Anglich moved behind Waltz and reached down under his coat into his breast pocket. He took a wallet out, shook out money, a driver's license, a police pistol permit, several insurance cards.

He put the stuff back, stared morosely at the desk, rubbed a thumbnail on his jaw. There was a shiny buff memo pad in front of him. Impressions of writing showed on the top blank sheet. He held it sideways against the light, then picked up a pencil and began to make light loose strokes across the paper. Writing came out dimly. When the sheet was shaded all over Pete Anglich read: 4623 Noon Street. Ask for Reno.

He tore the sheet off, folded it into a pocket, picked his gun up and crossed to the door. He reversed the key, locked the room from the outside, went back to the stairs and down them to the alley.

The body of the Negro lay as it had fallen, between the small sedan and the dark wall. The alley was empty. Pete Anglich stooped, searched the dead man's pockets, came up with a roll of money. He counted the money in the dim light of a match, separated eighty-seven dollars from what there was, and started to put the few remaining bills back. A piece of torn paper fluttered to the pavement. One side only was torn, jaggedly.

Pete Anglich crouched beside the car, struck another match, looked at a half-sheet from a buff memo pad on which was written, beginning with the tear:————t. Ask for Reno.

He clicked his teeth and let the match fall. "Better," he said softly.

He got into the car, started it and drove out of the alley.

## 7

The number was on a front-door transom, faintly lit from behind, the only light the house showed. It was a big frame house, in the block above where the stake-out had been. The windows in front were closely curtained. Noise came from behind them, voices and laughter, the high-pitched whine of a colored girl's singing. Cars were parked along the curb, on both sides of the street.

A tall thin Negro in dark clothes and gold nose-glasses opened the door. There was another door behind him, shut. He stood in a dark box between the two doors.

Pete Anglich said: "Reno?"

The tall Negro nodded, said nothing.

"I've come for the girl Rufe left, the white girl."

The tall Negro stood a moment quite motionless, looking over Pete Anglich's head. When he spoke, his voice was a lazy rustle of sound that seemed to come from somewhere else.

"Come in and shut the do'."

Pete Anglich stepped into the house, shut the outer door behind him. The tall Negro opened the inner door. It was thick, heavy. When he opened it sound and light jumped at them. A purplish light. He went through the inner door, into a hallway.

The purplish light came through a broad arch from a long living room. It had heavy velour drapes, davenports and deep chairs, a glass bar in the corner, and a white-coated Negro behind the bar. Four couples lounged about the room drinking; slim, slick-haired Negro sheiks and girls with bare arms, sheer silk legs, plucked eyebrows. The soft, purplish light made the scene unreal.

Reno stared vaguely past Pete Anglich's shoulder, dropped his heavy-lidded eyes, said wearily: "You says which?"

The Negroes beyond the arch were quiet, staring. The barman stooped and put his hands down under the bar.

Pete Anglich put his hand into his pocket slowly, brought out a crumpled piece of paper.

"This any help?"

Reno took the paper, studied it. He reached languidly into his vest and brought out another piece of the same color. He fitted the pieces together. His head went back and he looked at the ceiling.

"Who send you?"

"Trimmer."

"I don' like it," the tall Negro said. "He done write my name. I don' like that. That ain't sma't. Apa't from that I guess I check you."

He turned and started up a long, straight flight of stairs. Pete Anglich followed him. One of the Negro youths in the living room snickered loudly.

Reno stopped suddenly, turned and went back down the steps, through the arch. He went up to the snickerer.

"This is business," he said exhaustedly. "Ain't no white folks comin' heah. Git me?"

The boy who had laughed said, "Okey, Reno," and lifted a tall, misted glass.

Reno came up the stairs again, talking to himself. Along the upper hall were many closed doors. There was faint pink light from flame-colored wall lamps. At the end Reno took a key out and unlocked the door.

He stood aside. "Git her out," he said tersely. "I don' handle no white cargo heah."

Pete Anglich stepped past him into a bedroom. An orange floor lamp glowed in the far corner near a flounced, gaudy bed. The windows were shut, the air heavy, sickish.

Token Ware lay on her side on the bed, with her face to the wall, sobbing quietly.

Pete Anglich stepped to the side of the bed, touched her. She whirled, cringed. Her head jerked around at him, her eyes dilated, her mouth half open as if to yell.

"Hello, there," he said quietly, very gently. "I've been looking all over for you."

The girl stared back at him. Slowly all the fear went out of her face.

**8**

The *News* photographer held the flashbulb holder high up in his left hand, leaned down over his camera.

"Now, the smile, Mr. Vidaury," he said. "The sad one—that one that makes 'em pant."

Vidaury turned in the chair and set his profile. He smiled at the girl in the red hat, then turned his face to the camera with the smile still on.

The bulb flared and the shutter clicked.

"Not bad, Mr. Vidaury. I've seen you do better."

"I've been under a great strain," Vidaury said gently.

"I'll say. Acid in the face is no fun," the photographer said.

The girl in the red hat tittered, then coughed, behind a gauntleted glove with red stitching on the back.

The photographer packed his stuff together. He was an oldish man in shiny blue serge, with sad eyes. He shook his gray head and straightened his hat.

"No, acid in the puss is no fun," he said. "Well, I hope our boys can see you in the morning, Mr. Vidaury."

"Delighted," Vidaury said wearily. "Just tell them to ring me from the lobby before they come up. And have a drink on your way out."

"I'm crazy," the photographer said. "I don't drink."

He hoisted his camera bag over his shoulder and trudged down the room. A small Jap in a white coat appeared from nowhere and let him out, then went away.

"Acid in the puss," the girl in the red hat said. "Ha, ha, ha! That's positively excruciating, if a nice girl may say so. Can I have a drink?"

"Nobody's stopping you," Vidaury growled.

"Nobody ever did, sweets."

She walked sinuously over to a table with a square Chinese tray on it. She mixed a stiff one. Vidaury said half absently: "That should be all till morning. The *Bulletin,* the *Press-Tribune,* the three wire services, the *News.* Not bad."

"I'd call it a perfect score," the girl in the red hat said.

Vidaury scowled at her. "But nobody caught," he said softly, "except an innocent passer-by. *You* wouldn't know anything about this squeeze, would you, Irma?"

Her smile was lazy, but cold. "Me take you for a measly grand? Be your forty years plus, Johnny. I'm a home-run hitter, always."

Vidaury stood up and crossed the room to a carved wood cabinet, unlocked a small drawer and took a large ball of crystal out of it. He went back to his chair, sat down, and leaned forward, holding the ball in his palms and staring into it, almost vacantly.

The girl in the red hat watched him over the rim of her glass. Her eyes widened, got a little glassy.

"Hell! He's gone psychic on the folks," she breathed. She put her glass down with a sharp slap on the tray, drifted over to his side and leaned down. Her voice was cooing, edged. "Ever hear of senile decay, Johnny? It happens to exceptionally wicked men in their forties. They get ga-ga over flowers and toys, cut out paper dolls and play with glass balls . . . Can it, for God's sake, Johnny! You're not a punk yet."

Vidaury stared fixedly into the crystal ball. He breathed slowly, deeply.

The girl in the red hat leaned still closer to him. "Let's go riding, Johnny," she cooed. "I like the night air. It makes me remember my tonsils."

"I don't want to go riding," Vidaury said vaguely. "I—I feel something. Something imminent."

The girl bent suddenly and knocked the ball out of his hands. It thudded heavily on the floor, rolled sluggishly in the deep nap of the rug.

Vidaury shot to his feet, his face convulsed.

"I want to go riding, handsome," the girl said coolly. "It's a nice night, and you've got a nice car. So I want to go riding."

Vidaury stared at her with hate in his eyes. Slowly he smiled. The hate went away. He reached out and touched her lips with two fingers.

"Of course we'll go riding, baby," he said softly.

He got the ball, locked it up in the cabinet, went through an inner door. The girl in the red hat opened a bag and touched her lips with rouge, pursed them, made a face at herself in the mirror of her compact, found a rough wool coat in beige braided with red, and shrugged into it carefully, tossed a scarflike collar end over her shoulder.

Vidaury came back with a hat and coat on, a fringed muffler hanging down his coat.

They went down the room.

"Let's sneak out the back way," he said at the door. "In case any more newshawks are hanging around."

"Why, Johnny!" the girl in the red hat raised mocking eyebrows. "People saw me come in, saw me here. Surely you wouldn't want them to think your girl friend stayed the night?"

"Hell!" Vidaury said violently and wrenched the door open.

The telephone bell jangled back in the room. Vidaury swore again, took his hand from the door and stood waiting while the little Jap in the white jacket came in and answered the phone.

The boy put the phone down, smiled depracatingly and gestured with his hands.

"You take, prease? I not understand."

Vidaury walked back and lifted the instrument. He said, "Yes? This is John Vidaury." He listened.

Slowly his fingers tightened on the phone. His whole face tightened, got white. He said slowly, thickly: "Hold the line a minute."

He put the phone down on its side, put his hand down on the table and leaned on it. The girl in the red hat came up behind him.

"Bad news, handsome? You look like a washed egg."

Vidaury turned his head slowly and stared at her. "Get the hell out of here," he said tonelessly.

She laughed. He straightened, took a single long step and slapped her across the mouth, hard.

"I said, get the hell out of here," he repeated in an utterly dead voice.

She stopped laughing and touched her lips with fingers in the gauntleted glove. Her eyes were round, but not shocked.

"Why, Johnny. You sweep me right off my feet," she said wonderingly. "You're simply terrific. Of course I'll go."

She turned quickly, with a light toss of her head, went back along the room to the door, waved her hand, and went out.

Vidaury was not looking at her when she waved. He lifted the phone as soon as the door clicked shut after her, said into it grimly: "Get over here, Waltz—and get over here quick!"

He dropped the phone on its cradle, stood a moment blank-eyed. He went back through the inner door, reappeared in a moment without his hat and overcoat. He held a thick, short automatic in his hand. He slipped it nose-down into the inside breast pocket of his dinner jacket, lifted the phone again slowly, said into it coldly and firmly: "If a Mr. Anglich calls to see me, send him up. Anglich." He spelled the name out, put the phone down carefully, and sat down in the easy chair beside it.

He folded his arms and waited.

**9**

The white-jacketed Japanese boy opened the door, bobbed his head, smiled, hissed politely: "Ah, you come inside, prease. Quite so, prease."

Pete Anglich patted Token Ware's shoulder, pushed her through the door into the long, vivid room. She looked shabby and forlorn against the background of handsome furnishings. Her eyes were reddened from crying, her mouth was smeared.

The door shut behind them and the little Japanese stole away.

They went down the stretch of thick, noiseless carpet, past quiet brooding lamps, bookcases sunk into the wall, shelves of alabaster and ivory, and porcelain and jade knickknacks, a huge mirror framed in blue glass, and surrounded by a frieze of lovingly autographed photos, low tables with lounging chairs, high tables with flowers, more books, more chairs, more rugs—and Vidaury sitting remotely with a glass in his hand, staring at them coldly.

He moved his hand carelessly, looked the girl up and down.

"Ah, yes, the man the police had here. Of course. Something I can do for you? I heard they made a mistake."

Pete Anglich turned a chair a little, pushed Token Ware into it. She sat down slowly, stiffly, licked her lips and stared at Vidaury with a frozen fascination.

A touch of polite distaste curled Vidaury's lips. His eyes were watchful.

Pete Anglich sat down. He drew a stick of gum out of his pocket, unwrapped it, slid it between his teeth. He looked worn, battered, tired. There were dark bruises on the side of his face and on his neck. He still needed a shave.

He said slowly, "This is Miss Ware. The girl that was supposed to get your dough."

Vidaury stiffened. A hand holding a cigarette began to tap restlessly on the arm of his chair. He stared at the girl, but didn't say anything. She half smiled at him, then flushed.

Pete Anglich said: "I hang around Noon Street. I know the sharpshooters, know what kind of folks belong there and what kind don't. I saw this little girl in a lunchwagon on Noon Street this evening. She looked uneasy and she was watching the clock. She didn't belong. When she left I followed her."

Vidaury nodded slightly. A gray tip of ash fell off the end of his cigarette. He looked down at it vaguely, nodded again.

"She went up Noon Street," Pete Anglich said. "A bad street for a white girl. I found her hiding in a doorway. Then a big Duesenberg slid around the corner and doused lights, and your money was thrown out on the sidewalk. She was scared. She asked me to get it. I got it."

Vidaury said smoothly, not looking at the girl: "She doesn't look like a crook. Have you told the police about her? I suppose not, or you wouldn't be here."

Pete Anglich shook his head, ground the gum around in his jaws. "Tell the law? A couple of times nix. This is velvet for us. We want our cut."

Vidaury started violently, then he was very still. His hand stopped beating the chair arm. His face got cold and white and grim. Then he reached up inside his dinner jacket and quietly took the short automatic out, held it on his knees. He leaned forward a little and smiled.

"Blackmailers," he said gravely, "are always rather interesting. How much would your cut be—and what have you got to sell?"

Pete Anglich looked thoughtfully at the gun. His jaws moved easily, crunching the gum. His eyes were unworried.

"Silence," he said gravely. "Just silence."

Vidaury made a sharp sudden gesture with the gun. "Talk," he said. "And talk fast. I don't like silence."

Pete Anglich nodded, said: "The acid-throwing threats were just a dream. You didn't get any. The extortion attempt was a phony. A publicity stunt. That's all." He leaned back in his chair.

Vidaury looked down the room past Pete Anglich's shoulder. He started to smile, then his face got wooden.

Trimmer Waltz had slid into the room through an open side door. He had his big Savage in his hand. He came slowly along the carpet without sound. Pete Anglich and the girl didn't see him.

Pete Anglich said, "Phony all the way through. Just a build-up. Guessing? Sure I am, but look a minute, see how soft it was played first—and how tough it was played afterward, after I showed in it. The girl works for Trimmer Waltz at the Juggernaut. She's down and out, and she scares easily. So Waltz sends her on a caper like that. Why? Because she's supposed to be nabbed. The stake-out's all arranged. If she squawks about Waltz, he laughs it off, points to the fact that the plant was almost in his alley, that it was a small stake at best, and his joint's doing all right. He points to the fact that a dumb girl goes to get it, and would he, a smart guy, pull anything like that? Certainly not.

"The cops will half believe him, and you'll make a big gesture and refuse to prosecute the girl. If she doesn't spill, you'll refuse to prosecute anyway, and you'll get your publicity just the same, either way. You need it bad, because you're slipping, and you'll get it, and all it will cost you is what you pay Waltz—or that's what you think. Is that crazy? Is that too far for a Hollywood heel to stretch? Then tell me why no Feds were on the case. Because those lads would keep on digging until they found the mouse, and then you'd be up for obstructing justice. That's why. The local law don't give a damn. They're so used to movie build-ups they just yawn and turn over and go to sleep again."

Waltz was halfway down the room now. Vidaury didn't look at him. He looked at the girl, smiled at her faintly.

"Now, see how tough it was played after I got into it," Pete Anglich said. "I went to the Juggernaut and talked to the girl. Waltz got us into his office and a big ape that works for him damn near strangled me. When I came to I was in an apartment and a dead girl was there, and she was shot, and a bullet was gone from my gun. The gun was on the floor beside me, and I stank of gin, and a prowl car was booming around the corner. And Miss Ware here was locked up in a whore house on Noon Street.

"Why all that hard stuff? Because Waltz had a perfectly swell blackmail racket lined up for you, and he'd have bled you whiter than an angel's wing. As long as you had a dollar, half of it would have been his. And you'd have paid it and liked it, Vidaury. You'd have had publicity, and you'd have had protection, but how you'd have paid for it!"

Waltz was close now, almost too close. Vidaury stood up suddenly. The short gun jerked at Pete Anglich's chest. Vidaury's voice was thin, an old man's voice. He said dreamily: "Take him, Waltz. I'm too jittery for this sort of thing."

Pete Anglich didn't even turn. His face became the face of a wooden Indian.

Waltz put his gun into Pete Anglich's back. He stood there half smiling, with the gun against Pete Anglich's back, looking across his shoulder at Vidaury.

"Dumb, Pete," he said dryly. "You had enough evening already. You ought to have stayed away from here—but I figured you couldn't pass it up."

Vidaury moved a little to one side, spread his legs, flattened his feet to the floor. There was a queer, greenish tint to his handsome face, a sick glitter in his deep eyes.

Token Ware stared at Waltz. Her eyes glittered with

panic, the lids straining away from the eyeballs, showing the whites all around the iris.

Waltz said, "I can't do anything here, Vidaury. I'd rather not walk him out alone, either. Get your hat and coat."

Vidaury nodded very slightly. His head just barely moved. His eyes were still sick.

"What about the girl?" he asked whisperingly.

Waltz grinned, shook his head, pressed the gun hard into Pete Anglich's back.

Vidaury moved a little more to the side, spread his feet again. The thick gun was very steady in his hand, but not pointed at anything in particular.

He closed his eyes, held them shut a brief instant, then opened them wide. He said slowly, carefully: "It looked all right as it was planned. Things just as far-fetched, just as unscrupulous, have been done before in Hollywood, often. I just didn't expect it to lead to hurting people, to killing. I'm—I'm just not enough of a heel to go on with it, Waltz. Not any further. You'd better put your gun up and leave."

Waltz shook his head; smiled a peculiar strained smile. He stepped back from Pete Anglich and held the Savage a little to one side.

"The cards are dealt," he said coldly. "You'll play 'em. Get going."

Vidaury sighed, sagged a little. Suddenly he was a lonely, forlorn man, no longer young.

"No," he said softly. "I'm through. The last flicker of a not-so-good reputation. It's my show, after all. Always the ham, but still my show. Put the gun up, Waltz. Take the air."

Waltz's face got cold and hard and expressionless. His eyes became the expressionless eyes of the killer. He moved the Savage a little more.

"Get—your—hat, Vidaury," he said very clearly.

"Sorry," Vidaury said, and fired.

Waltz's gun flamed at the same instant, the two

explosions blended. Vidaury staggered to his left and half turned, then straightened his body again.

He looked steadily at Waltz. "Beginner's luck," he said, and waited.

Pete Anglich had his Colt out now, but he didn't need it. Waltz fell slowly on his side. His cheek and the side of his big-veined nose pressed the nap of the rug. He moved his left arm a little, tried to throw it over his back. He gurgled, then was still.

Pete Anglich kicked the Savage away from Waltz's sprawled body.

Vidaury asked draggingly: "Is he dead?"

Pete Anglich grunted, didn't answer. He looked at the girl. She was standing up with her back against the telephone table, the back of her hand to her mouth in the conventional attitude of startled horror. So conventional it looked silly.

Pete Anglich looked at Vidaury. He said sourly: "Beginner's luck—yeah. But suppose you'd missed him? He was bluffing. Just wanted you in a little deeper, so you wouldn't squawk. As a matter of fact, I'm his alibi on a kill."

Vidaury said: "Sorry ... I'm sorry." He sat down suddenly, leaned his head back and closed his eyes.

"God, but he's handsome!" Token Ware said reverently. "And brave."

Vidaury put his hand to his left shoulder, pressed it hard against his body. Blood oozed slowly between his fingers. Token Ware let out a stifled screech.

Pete Anglich looked down the room. The little Jap in the white coat had crept into the end of it, stood silently, a small huddled figure against the wall. Pete Anglich looked at Vidaury again. Very slowly, as though unwillingly, he said: "Miss Ware has folks in 'Frisco. You can send her home, with a little present. That's natural—and open. She turned Waltz up to me. That's how I came into it. I told him you were wise and he came here to shut you up. Tough-guy stuff. The coppers will laugh at it, but they'll laugh in their cuffs. After all, they're getting publicity too. The phony angle is out. Check?"

Vidaury opened his eyes, said faintly, "You're— you're very decent about it. I won't forget." His head lolled.

"He's fainted," the girl cried.

"So he has," Pete Anglich said. "Give him a nice big kiss and he'll snap out of it . . . And you'll have something to remember all your life."

He ground his teeth, went to the phone, and lifted it.

**SMART-ALECK
KILL**

THE DOORMAN of the Kilmarnock was six foot two. He wore a pale blue uniform, and white gloves made his hands look enormous. He opened the door of the Yellow taxi as gently as an old maid stroking a cat.

Johnny Dalmas got out and turned to the red-haired driver. He said: "Better wait for me around the corner, Joey."

The driver nodded, tucked a toothpick a little farther back in the corner of his mouth, and swung his cab expertly away from the white-marked loading zone. Dalmas crossed the sunny sidewalk and went into the enormous cool lobby of the Kilmarnock. The carpets were thick, soundless. Bellboys stood with folded arms and the two clerks behind the marble desk looked austere.

Dalmas went across to the elevator lobby. He got into a paneled car and said: "End of the line, please."

The penthouse floor had a small quiet lobby with three doors opening off it, one to each wall. Dalmas crossed to one of them and rang the bell.

Derek Walden opened the door. He was about forty-five, possibly a little more, and had a lot of powdery gray hair and a handsome, dissipated face that was beginning to go pouchy. He had on a monogrammed

51

lounging robe and a glass full of whiskey in his hand. He was a little drunk.

He said thickly, morosely: "Oh, it's you. C'mon in, Dalmas."

He went back into the apartment, leaving the door open. Dalmas shut it and followed him into a long, high-ceilinged room with a balcony at one end and a line of french windows along the left side. There was a terrace outside.

Derek Walden sat down in a brown and gold chair against the wall and stretched his legs across a foot stool. He swirled the whiskey around in his glass, looking down at it.

"What's on your mind?" he asked.

Dalmas stared at him a little grimly. After a moment he said: "I dropped in to tell you I'm giving you back your job."

Walden drank the whiskey out of his glass and put it down on the corner of a table. He fumbled around for a cigarette, stuck it in his mouth and forgot to light it.

"Tha' so?" His voice was blurred but indifferent.

Dalmas turned away from him and walked over to one of the windows. It was open and an awning flapped outside. The traffic noise from the boulevard was faint.

He spoke over his shoulder:

"The investigation isn't getting anywhere—because you don't want it to get anywhere. *You* know why you're being blackmailed. *I* don't. Eclipse Films is interested because they have a lot of sugar tied up in film you have made."

"To hell with Eclipse Films," Walden said, almost quitely.

Dalmas shook his head and turned around. "Not from my angle. They stand to lose if you get in a jam the publicity hounds can't handle. You took me on because you were asked to. It was a waste of time. You haven't cooperated worth a cent."

Walden said in an unpleasant tone: "I'm handling this

my own way and I'm not gettin' into any jam. I'll make my own deal—when I can buy something that'll stay bought . . . And all you have to do is make the Eclipse people think the situation's bein' taken care of. That clear?"

Dalmas came partway back across the room. He stood with one hand on top of a table, beside an ash tray littered with cigarette stubs that had very dark lip rouge on them. He looked down at these absently.

"That wasn't explained to me, Walden," he said coldly.

"I thought you were smart enough to figure it out," Walden sneered. He leaned sidewise and slopped some more whiskey into his glass. "Have a drink?"

Dalmas said: "No, thanks."

Walden found the cigarette in his mouth and threw it on the floor. He drank. "What the hell!" he snorted. "You're a private detective and you're being paid to make a few motions that don't mean anything. It's a clean job—as your racket goes."

Dalmas said: "That's another crack I could do without hearing."

Walden made an abrupt, angry motion. His eyes glittered. The corners of his mouth drew down and his face got sulky. He avoided Dalmas' stare.

Dalmas said: "I'm not against you, but I never was for you. You're not the kind of guy I could go for, ever. If you had played with me, I'd have done what I could. I still will—but not for your sake. I don't want your money—and you can pull your shadows off my tail any time you like."

Walden put his feet on the floor. He laid his glass down very carefully on the table at his elbow. The whole expression of his face changed.

"Shadows? . . . I don't get you." He swallowed. "I'm not having you shadowed."

Dalmas stared at him. After a moment he nodded. "Okey, then. I'll backtrack on the next one and see if I can make him tell who he's working for . . . I'll find out."

Walden said very quietly: "I wouldn't do that, if I were you. You're—you're monkeying with people that might get nasty . . . I know what I'm talking about."

"That's something I'm not going to let worry me," Dalmas said evenly. "If it's the people that want *your* money, they were nasty a long time ago."

He held his hat out in front of him and looked at it. Walden's face glistened with sweat. His eyes looked sick. He opened his mouth to say something.

The door buzzer sounded.

Walden scowled quickly, swore. He stared down the room but did not move.

"Too damn many people come here without bein' announced," he growled. "My Jap boy is off for the day."

The buzzer sounded again, and Walden started to get up. Dalmas said: "I'll see what it is. I'm on my way anyhow."

He nodded to Walden, went down the room and opened the door.

Two men came in with guns in their hands. One of the guns dug sharply into Dalmas' ribs, and the man who was holding it said urgently: "Back up, and make it snappy. This is one of those stick-ups you read about."

He was dark and good-looking and cheerful. His face was as clear as a cameo, almost without hardness. He smiled.

The one behind him was short and sandy-haired. He scowled. The dark one said: "This is Walden's dick, Noddy. Take him over and go through him for a gun."

The sandy-haired man, Noddy, put a short-barreled revolver against Dalmas' stomach and his partner kicked the door shut, then strolled carelessly down the room toward Walden.

Noddy took a .38 Colt from under Dalmas' arm, walked around him and tapped his pockets. He put his

own gun away and transferred Dalmas' Colt to his
business hand.

"Okey, Ricchio. This one's clean," he said in a
grumbling voice. Dalmas let his arms fall, turned and
went back into the room. He looked thoughtfully at
Walden. Walden was leaning forward with his mouth
open and an expression of intense concentration on his
face. Dalmas looked at the dark stick-up and said softly:
"Ricchio?"

The dark boy glanced at him. "Over there by the
table, sweetheart. I'll do all the talkin'."

Walden made a hoarse sound in his throat. Ricchio
stood in front of him, looking down at him pleasantly,
his gun dangling from one finger by the trigger guard.

"You're too slow on the pay-off, Walden. Too damn
slow! So we came to tell you about it. Tailed your dick
here too. Wasn't that cute?"

Dalmas said gravely, quietly: "This punk used to be
your bodyguard, Walden—if his name is Ricchio."

Walden nodded silently and licked his lips. Ricchio
snarled at Dalmas: "Don't crack wise, dick. I'm tellin'
you again." He stared with hot eyes, then looked back
at Walden, looked at a watch on his wrist.

"It's eight minutes past three, Walden. I figure a guy
with your drag can still get dough out of the bank.
We're giving you an hour to raise ten grand. Just an
hour. And we're takin' your shamus along to arrange
about delivery."

Walden nodded again, still silent. He put his hands
down on his knees and clutched them until his knuckles
whitened.

Ricchio went on: "We'll play clean. Our racket
wouldn't be worth a squashed bug if we didn't. You'll
play clean too. If you don't your shamus will wake up
on a pile of dirt. Only he won't wake up. Get it?"

Dalmas said contemptuously: "And if he pays up—I
suppose you turn me loose to put the finger on you."

Smoothly, without looking at him, Ricchio said:

"There's an answer to that one, too ... Ten grand today, Walden. The other ten the first of the week. Unless we have trouble. ... If we do, we'll get paid for our trouble."

Walden made an aimless, defeated gesture with both hands outspread. "I guess I can arrange it," he said hurriedly.

"Swell. We'll be on our way then."

Ricchio nodded shortly and put his gun away. He took a brown kid glove out of his pocket, put it on his right hand, moved across then took Dalmas' Colt away from the sandy-haired man. He looked it over, slipped it into his side pocket and held it there with the gloved hand.

"Let's drift," he said with a jerk of his head.

They went out. Derek Walden stared after them bleakly.

The elevator car was empty except for the operator. They got off at the mezzanine and went across a silent writing room past a stained-glass window with lights behind it to give the effect of sunshine. Ricchio walked half a step behind on Dalmas' left. The sandy-haired man was on his right, crowding him.

They went down carpeted steps to an arcade of luxury shops, along that, out of the hotel through the side entrance. A small brown sedan was parked across the street. The sandy-haired man slid behind the wheel, stuck his gun under his leg and stepped on the starter. Ricchio and Dalmas got in the back. Ricchio drawled: "East on the boulevard, Noddy. I've got to figure."

Noddy grunted. "That's a kick," he growled over his shoulder. "Ridin' a guy down Wilshire in daylight."

"Drive the heap, bozo."

The sandy-haired man grunted again and drove the small sedan away from the curb, slowed a moment later for the boulevard stop. An empty Yellow pulled away from the west curb, swung around in the middle of the block and fell in behind. Noddy made his stop, turned right and went on. The taxi did the same. Ricchio glanced back at it without interest. There was a lot of traffic on Wilshire.

Dalmas leaned back against the upholstery and said thoughtfully: "Why wouldn't Walden use his telephone while we were coming down?"

Ricchio smiled at him. He took his hat off and dropped it in his lap, then took his right hand out of his pocket and held it under the hat with the gun in it.

"He wouldn't want us to get mad at him, dick."

"So he lets a couple of punks take me for the ride."

Ricchio said coldly: "It's not that kind of a ride. We need you in our business . . . And we ain't punks, see?"

Dalmas rubbed his jaw with a couple of fingers. He smiled quickly and snapped: "Straight ahead at Robertson?"

"Yeah. I'm still figuring," Ricchio said.

"What a brain!" the sandy-haired man sneered.

Ricchio grinned tightly and showed even white teeth. The light changed to red half a block ahead. Noddy slid the sedan forward and was first in the line at the intersection. The empty Yellow drifted up on his left. Not quite level. The driver of it had red hair. His cap was balanced on one side of his head and he whistled cheerfully past a toothpick.

Dalmas drew his feet back against the seat and put his weight on them. He pressed his back hard against the upholstery. The tall traffic light went green and the sedan started forward, then hung a moment for a car that crowded into a fast left turn. The Yellow slipped forward on the left and the red-haired driver leaned over his wheel, yanked it suddenly to the right. There was a grinding, tearing noise. The riveted fender of the taxi plowed over the low-swung fender of the brown sedan, locked over its left front wheel. The two cars jolted to a stop.

Horn blasts behind the two cars sounded angrily, impatiently.

Dalmas' right fist crashed against Ricchio's jaw. His left hand closed over the gun in Ricchio's lap. He jerked it loose as Ricchio sagged in the corner. Ricchio's head wobbled. His eyes opened and shut flickeringly. Dalmas slid away from him along the seat and slipped the Colt under his arm.

Noddy was sitting quite still in the front seat. His right hand moved slowly towards the gun under his thigh. Dalmas opened the door of the sedan and got out, shut the door, took two steps and opened the door of the taxi. He stood beside the taxi and watched the sandy-haired man.

Horns of the stalled cars blared furiously. The driver of the Yellow was out in front tugging at the two cars with a great show of energy and with no result at all. His toothpick waggled up and down in his mouth. A motorcycle officer in amber glasses threaded the traffic, looked the situation over wearily, jerked his head at the driver.

"Get in and back up," he advised. "Argue it out somewhere else—we use this intersection."

The driver grinned and scuttled around the front end of his Yellow. He climbed into it, threw it in gear and worried it backwards with a lot of tooting and armwaving. It came clear. The sandy-haired man peered woodenly from the sedan. Dalmas got into the taxi and pulled the door shut.

The motorcycle officer drew a whistle out and blew two sharp blasts on it, spread his arms from east to west. The brown sedan went through the intersection like a cat chased by a police dog.

The Yellow went after it. Half a block on, Dalmas leaned forward and tapped on the glass.

"Let 'em go, Joey. You can't catch them and I don't want them . . . That was a swell routine back there."

The redhead leaned his chin towards the opening in the panel. "Cinch, chief," he said, grinning. "Try me on a hard one some time."

## 2

The telephone rang at twenty minutes to five. Dalmas was lying on his back on the bed. He was in his room at the Merrivale. He reached for the phone without looking at it, said: "Hello."

The girl's voice was pleasant and a little strained. "This is Mianne Crayle. Remember?"

Dalmas took a cigarette from between his lips. "Yes, Miss Crayle."

"Listen. You must please go over and see Derek Walden. He's worried stiff about something and he's drinking himself blind. Something's got to be done."

Dalmas stared past the phone at the ceiling. The hand holding his cigarette beat a tattoo on the side of the bed. He said slowly: "He doesn't answer his phone, Miss Crayle. I've tried to call him a time or two."

There was a short silence at the other end of the line. Then the voice said: "I left my key under the door. You'd better just go on in."

Dalmas' eyes narrowed. The fingers of his right hand became still. He said slowly: "I'll get over there right away, Miss Crayle. Where can I reach you?"

"I'm not sure . . . At John Sutro's, perhaps. We were supposed to go there."

Dalmas said: "That's fine." He waited for the click, then hung up and put the phone away on the night table. He sat up on the side of the bed and stared at a patch of sunlight on the wall for a minute or two. Then he shrugged, stood up. He finished a drink that stood beside the telephone, put on his hat, went down in the elevator and go into the second taxi in the line outside the hotel.

"Kilmarnock again, Joey. Step on it."

It took fifteen minutes to get to Kilmarnock.

The tea dance had let out and the streets around the big hotel were a mess of cars bucking their way out from the three entrances. Dalmas got out of the taxi half a block away and walked past groups of flushed débutantes and their escorts to the arcade entrance. He went in, walked up the stairs to the mezzanine, crossed the writing room and got into an elevator full of people. They all got out before the penthouse floor.

Dalmas rang Walden's bell twice. Then he bent over and looked under the door. There was a fine thread of light broken by an obstruction. He looked back at the elevator indicators, then stooped and teased something out from under the door with the blade of a penknife. It was a flat key. He went in with it ... stopped ... stared ...

There was death in the big room. Dalmas went towards it slowly, walking softly, listening. There was a hard light in his gray eyes and the bone of his jaw made a sharp line that was pale against the tan of his cheek.

Derek Walden was slumped almost casually in the brown and gold chair. His mouth was slightly open. There was a blackened hole in his right temple, and a lacy pattern of blood spread down the side of his face and across the hollow of his neck as far as the soft collar of his shirt. His right hand trailed in the thick nap of the rug. The fingers held a small, black automatic.

The daylight was beginning to fade in the room. Dalmas stood perfectly still and stared at Derek Walden for a long time. There was no sound anywhere. The breeze had gone down and the awnings outside the french windows were still.

Dalmas took a pair of thin suede gloves from his left hip pocket and drew them on. He kneeled on the rug beside Walden and gently eased the gun from the clasp of his stiffening fingers. It was a .32, with a walnut grip, a black finish. He turned it over and looked at the stock. His mouth tightened. The number had been filed off and the patch of file marks glistened faintly against the dull black of the finish. He put the gun down on the rug and stood up, walked slowly towards the telephone that was on the end of a library table, beside a flat bowl of cut flowers.

He put his hand towards the phone but didn't touch it. He let the hand fall to his side. He stood there a moment, then turned and went quickly back and picked up the gun again. He slipped the magazine out and ejected the shell that was in the breech, picked that up and pressed it into the magazine. He forked two fingers of his left hand over the barrel, held the cocking piece back, twisted the breech block and broke the gun apart. He took the butt piece over to the window.

The number that was duplicated on the inside of the stock had not been filed off.

He reassembled the gun quickly, put the empty shell into the chamber, pushed the magazine home, cocked the gun and fitted it back into Derek Walden's dead hand. He pulled the suede gloves off his hands and wrote the number down in a small notebook.

He left the apartment, went down in the elevator, left the hotel. It was half-past five and some of the cars on the boulevard had switched on their lights.

## 3

The blond man who opened the door at Sutro's did it very thoroughly. The door crashed back against the wall and the blond man sat down on the floor—still holding on to the knob. He said indignantly: "Earthquake, by gad!"

Dalmas looked down at him without amusement.

"Is Miss Mianne Crayle here—or wouldn't you know?" he asked.

The blond man got off the floor and hurled the door away from him. It went shut with another crash. He said in a loud voice: "Everybody's here but the Pope's tomcat—and he's expected."

Dalmas nodded. "You ought to have a swell party."

He went past the blond man down the hall and turned under an arch into a big old-fashioned room with built-in china closets and a lot of shabby furniture. There were seven or eight people in the room and they were all flushed with liquor.

A girl in shorts and a green polo shirt was shooting craps on the floor with a man in dinner clothes. A fat man with nose-glasses was talking sternly into a toy telephone. He was saying: "Long Distance—Sioux City —and put some snap into it, sister!"

The radio blared "Sweet Madness."

Two couples were dancing around carelessly bumping into each other and the furniture. A man who looked like Al Smith was dancing all alone, with a drink in his hand and an absent expression on his face. A tall, white-faced blonde weaved towards Dalmas, slopping liquor out of her glass. She shrieked: "Darling! Fancy meeting you here!"

Dalmas went around her, went towards a saffron-colored woman who had just come into the room with a bottle of gin in each hand. She put the bottles on the piano and leaned against it, looking bored. Dalmas went up to her and asked for Miss Crayle.

The saffron-colored woman reached a cigarette out of an open box on the piano. "Outside—in the yard," she said tonelessly.

Dalmas said: "Thank you, Mrs. Sutro."

She stared at him blankly. He went under another arch, into a darkened room with wicker furniture in it. A door led to a glassed-in porch and a door out of that led down steps to a path that wound off through dim trees. Dalmas followed the path to the edge of a bluff that looked out over the lighted part of Hollywood. There was a stone seat at the edge of the bluff. A girl sat on it with her back to the house. A cigarette tip glowed in the darkness. She turned her head slowly and stood up.

She was small and dark and delicately made. Her

mouth showed dark with rouge, but there was not enough light to see her face clearly. Her eyes were shadowed.

Dalmas said: "I have a cab outside, Miss Crayle. Or did you bring a car?"

"No car. Let's go. It's rotten here, and I don't drink gin."

They went back along the path and passed around the side of the house. A trellis-topped gate let them out on the sidewalk, and they went along by the fence to where the taxi was waiting. The driver was leaning against it with one heel hooked on the edge of the running board. He opened the cab door. They got in.

Dalmas said: "Stop at a drugstore for some butts, Joey."

"Oke."

Joey slid behind his wheel and started up. The cab went down a steep, winding hill. There was a little moisture on the surface of the asphalt pavement and the store fronts echoed back the swishing sound of the tires.

After a while Dalmas said: "What time did you leave Walden?"

The girl spoke without turning her head towards him. "About three o'clock."

"Put it a little later, Miss Crayle. He was alive at three o'clock—and there was somebody else with him."

The girl made a small, miserable sound like a strangled sob. Then, she said very softly: "I know . . . he's dead." She lifted her gloved hands and pressed them against her temples.

Dalmas said: "Sure. Let's not get any more tricky than we have to . . . Maybe we'll have to—enough."

She said very slowly, in a low voice: "I was there after he was dead."

Dalmas nodded. He did not look at her. The cab went on and after a while it stopped in front of a corner drugstore. The driver turned in his seat and looked back. Dalmas stared at him, but spoke to the girl.

"You ought to have told me more over the phone. I might have got in a hell of a jam. I may be in a hell of a jam now."

The girl swayed forward and started to fall. Dalmas put his arm out quickly and caught her, pushed her back against the cushions. Her head wobbled on her shoulders and her mouth was a dark gash in her stone-white face. Dalmas held her shoulder and felt her pulse with his free hand. He said sharply, grimly: "Let's go on to Carli's, Joey. Never mind the butts . . . This party has to have a drink—in a hurry."

Joey slammed the cab in gear and stepped on the accelerator.

## 4

Carli's was a small club at the end of a passage between a sporting-goods store and a circulating library. There was a grilled door and a man behind it who had given up trying to look as if it mattered who came in.

Dalmas and the girl sat in a small booth with hard seats and looped-back green curtains. There were high partitions between the booths. There was a long bar down the other side of the room and a big juke box at the end of it. Now and then, when there wasn't enough noise, the bartender put a nickel in the juke box.

The waiter put two small glasses of brandy on the table and Mianne Crayle downed hers at a gulp. A little light came into her shadowed eyes. She peeled a black and white gauntlet off her right hand and sat playing with the empty fingers of it, staring down at the table. After a little while the waiter came back with a couple of brandy highballs.

When he had gone away again Mianne Crayle began to speak in a low, clear voice, without raising her head:

"I wasn't the first of his women by several dozen. I wouldn't have been the last—by that many more. But he had his decent side. And believe it or not he didn't pay my room rent."

Dalmas nodded, didn't say anything. The girl went on without looking at him: "He was a heel in a lot of ways. When he was sober he had the dark blue sulks. When he was lit up he was vile. When he was nicely edged he was a pretty good sort of guy besides being the best smut director in Hollywood. He could get more smooth sexy tripe past the Hays office than any other three men."

Dalmas said without expression: "He was on his way out. Smut is on its way out, and that was all he knew."

The girl looked at him briefly, lowered her eyes again and drank a little of her highball. She took a tiny handkerchief out of the pocket of her sports jacket and patted her lips.

The people on the other side of the partition were making a great deal of noise.

Mianne Crayle said: "We had lunch on the balcony. Derek was drunk and on the way to get drunker. He had something on his mind. Something that worried him a lot."

Dalmas smiled faintly. "Maybe it was the twenty grand somebody was trying to pry loose from him—or didn't you know about that?"

"It might have been that. Derek was a bit tight about money."

"His liquor cost him a lot," Dalmas said dryly. "And that motor cruiser he liked to play about in—down below the border."

The girl lifted her head with a quick jerk. There were sharp lights of pain in her dark eyes. She said very slowly: "He bought all his liquor at Ensenada. Brought it in himself. He had to be careful—with the quantity he put away."

Dalmas nodded. A cold smile played about the corners of his mouth. He finished his drink and put a cigarette in his mouth, felt in his pocket for a match. The holder on the table was empty.

"Finish your story, Miss Crayle," he said.

"We went up to the apartment. He got two fresh bottles out and said he was going to get good and drunk ... Then we quarreled ... I couldn't stand any more of it. I went away. When I got home I began to worry about him. I called up but he wouldn't answer the phone. I went back finally ... and let myself in with the key I had ... and he was dead in the chair."

After a moment Dalmas said: "Why didn't you tell me some of that over the phone?"

She pressed the heels of her hands together, said very softly: "I was terribly afraid ... And there was something ... wrong."

Dalmas put his head back against the partition, stared at her with his eyes half closed.

"It's an old gag," she said. "I'm almost ashamed to spring it. But Derek Walden was left-handed ... I'd know about that, wouldn't I?"

Dalmas said very softly: "A lot of people must have known that—but one of them might have got careless."

Dalmas stared at Mianne Crayle's empty glove. She was twisting it between her fingers.

"Walden was left-handed," he said slowly. "That means he didn't suicide. The gun was in his other hand. There was no sign of a struggle and the hole in his temple was powder-burned, looked as if the shot came from about the right angle. That means whoever shot him was someone who could get in there and get close to him. Or else he was paralyzed drunk, and in that case whoever did it had to have a key."

Mianne Crayle pushed the glove away from her. She clenched her hands. "Don't make it any plainer," she said sharply. "I know the police will think I did it. Well—I didn't. I loved the poor damn fool. What do you think of that?"

Dalmas said without emotion: "You *could* have done it, Miss Crayle. They'll think of that, won't they? And you might be smart enough to act the way you have afterwards. They'll think of that, too."

"That wouldn't be smart," she said bitterly. "Just smart-aleck."

"Smart-aleck kill!" Dalmas laughed grimly. "Not bad." He ran his fingers through his crisp hair. "No, I don't think we can pin it on you—and maybe the cops won't know he was left-handed . . . until somebody else gets a chance to find things out."

He leaned over the table a little, put his hands on the edge as if to get up. His eyes narrowed thoughtfully on her face.

"There's one man downtown that might give me a break. He's all cop, but he's an old guy and don't give a damn about his publicity. Maybe if you went down with me, let him size you up and hear the story, he'd stall the case a few hours and hold out on the papers."

He looked at her questioningly. She drew her glove on and said quietly: "Let's go."

## 5

When the elevator doors at the Merrivale closed, the big man put his newspaper down from in front of his face and yawned. He got up slowly from the settee in the corner and loafed across the small but sedate lobby. He squeezed himself into a booth at the end of a row of house phones. He dropped a coin in the slot and dialed with a thick forefinger, forming the number with his lips.

After a pause he leaned close to the mouthpiece and said: "This is Denny. I'm at the Merrivale. Our man just came in. I lost him outside and came here to wait for him to get back."

He had a heavy voice with a burr in it. He listened

to the voice at the other end, nodded and hung up without saying anything more. He went out of the booth, crossed to the elevators. On the way he dropped a cigar butt into a glazed jar full of white sand.

In the elevator he said: "Ten," and took his hat off. He had straight black hair that was damp with perspiration, a wide, flat face and small eyes. His clothes were unpressed, but not shabby. He was a studio dick and he worked for Eclipse Films.

He got out at the tenth floor and went along a dim corridor, turned a corner and knocked at a door. There was a sound of steps inside. The door opened. Dalmas opened it.

The big man went in, dropped his hat casually on the bed, sat down in an easy chair by the window without being asked.

He said: "Hi, boy. I hear you need some help."

Dalmas looked at him for a moment without answering. Then he said slowly, frowningly: "Maybe—for a tail. I asked for Collins. I thought you'd be too easy to spot."

He turned away and went into the bathroom, came out with two glasses. He mixed the drinks on the bureau, handed one. The big man drank, smacked his lips and put his glass down on the sill of the open window. He took a short, chubby cigar out of his vest pocket.

"Collins wasn't around," he said. "And I was just countin' my thumbs. So the big cheese give me the job. Is it footwork?"

"I don't know. Probably not," Dalmas said indifferently.

"If it's a tail in a car, I'm okey. I brought my little coupe."

Dalmas took his glass and sat down on the side of the bed. He stared at the big man with a faint smile. The big man bit the end off his cigar and spit it out.

Then he bent over and picked up the piece, looked at it, tossed it out of the window.

"It's a swell night. A bit warm for so late in the year," he said.

Dalmas said slowly: "How well do you know Derek Walden, Denny?"

Denny looked out of the window. There was a sort of haze in the sky and the reflection of a red neon sign behind a nearby building looked like a fire.

He said: "I don't what you call know him. I've seen him around. I know he's one of the big money guys on the lot."

"Then you won't fall over if I tell you he's dead," Dalmas said evenly.

Denny turned around slowly. The cigar, still unlighted, moved up and down in his wide mouth. He looked mildly interested.

Dalmas went on: "It's a funny one. A blackmail gang has been working on him, Denny. Looks like it got his goat. He's dead—with a hole in his head and a gun in his hand. It happened this afternoon."

Denny opened his small eyes a little wider. Dalmas sipped his drink and rested the glass on his thigh.

"His girl friend found him. She had a key to the apartment in the Kilmarnock. The Jap boy was away and that's all the help he kept. The gal didn't tell anyone. She beat it and called me up. I went over . . . I didn't tell anybody either."

The big man said very slowly: "For Pete's sake! The cops'll stick it into you and break it off, brother. You can't get away with that stuff."

Dalmas stared at him, then turned his head away and stared at a picture on the wall. He said coldly: "I'm doing it—and you're helping me. We've got a job, and a damn powerful organization behind us. There's a lot of sugar at stake."

"How do you figure?" Denny asked grimly. He didn't look pleased.

"The girl friend doesn't think Walden suicided, Denny. I don't either, and I've got a sort of lead. But it has to be worked fast, because it's as good a lead for the law as us. I didn't expect to be able to check it right away, but I got a break."

Denny said: "Uh-huh. Don't make it too clever. I'm a slow thinker."

He struck a match and lit his cigar. His hand shook just a little.

Dalmas said: "It's not clever. It's kind of dumb. The gun that killed Walden is a filed gun. But I broke it and the inside number wasn't filed. And Headquarters has the number, in the special permits."

"And you just went in and asked for it and they gave it to you," Denny said grimly. "And when they pick Walden up and trace the gun themselves, they'll just think it was swell of you to beat them to it." He made a harsh noise in his throat.

Dalmas said: "Take it easy, boy. The guy that did the checking rates. I don't have to worry about that."

"Like hell you don't! And what would a guy like Walden be doin' with a filed gun? That's a felony rap."

Dalmas finished his drink and carried his empty glass over to the bureau. He held the whiskey bottle out. Denny shook his head. He looked very disgusted.

"If he had the gun, he might not have known about that, Denny. And it could be that it wasn't his gun at all. If it was a killer's gun, then the killer was an amateur. A professional wouldn't have that kind of artillery."

The big man said slowly: "Okey, what you get on the rod?"

Dalmas sat down on the bed again. He dug a package of cigarettes out of his pocket, lit one, and leaned forward to toss the match through the open window. He said: "The permit was issued about a year go to a newshawk on the Press-Chronicle, name of Dart Burwand. This Burwand was bumped off last April on the ramp of the Arcade Depot. He was all set to leave town, but he didn't make it. They never cracked the case, but the hunch is that this Burwand was tied to some racket —like the Lingle killing in Chi—and that he tried to shake one of the big boys. The big boy backfired on the idea. Exit Burwand."

The big man was breathing deeply. He had let his cigar go out. Dalmas watched him gravely while he talked.

"I got that from Westfalls, on the Press-Chronicle," Dalmas said. "He's a friend of mine. There's more of it. This gun was given back to Burwand's wife— probably. She still lives here—out on North Kenmore. She might tell me what she did with the gun . . . and she might be tied to some racket herself, Denny. In that case she wouldn't tell me, but after I talk to her she might make some contacts we ought to know about. Get the idea?"

Denny struck another match and held it on the end of his cigar. His voice said thickly: "What do I do—tail the broad after you put the idea to her, about the gun?"

"Right."

The big man stood up, pretended to yawn. "Can do," he grunted. "But why all the hush-hush about Walden? Why not let the cops work it out? We're just goin' to get ourselves a lot of bad marks at Headquarters."

Dalmas said slowly: "It's got to be risked. We don't know what the blackmail crowd had on Walden, and the studio stands to lose too much money if it comes out in the investigation and gets a front-page spread all over the country."

Denny said: "You talk like Walden was spelled Valentino. Hell, the guy's only a director. All they got to do is take his name off a couple of unreleased pictures."

"They figure different," Dalmas said. "But maybe that's because they haven't talked to you."

Denny said roughly: "Okey. But me, I'd let the girl

friend take the damn rap! All the law ever wants is a
fall guy."

He went around the bed to get his hat, crammed it
on his head.

"Swell," he said sourly. "We gotta find out all about
it before the cops even know Walden is dead." He
gestured with one hand and laughed mirthlessly. "Like
they do in the movies."

Dalmas put the whiskey bottle away in the bureau
drawer and put his hat on. He opened the door and
stood aside for Denny to go out. He switched off the
lights.

It was ten minutes to nine.

## 6

The tall blonde looked at Dalmas out of greenish eyes
with very small pupils. He went in past her quickly,
without seeming to move quickly. He pushed the door
shut with his elbow.

He said: "I'm a dick—private—Mrs. Burwand. Trying to dig up a little dope you might know about."

The blonde said: "The name is Dalton, Helen Dalton.
Forget the Burwand stuff."

Dalmas smiled and said: "I'm sorry. I should have
known."

The blonde shrugged her shoulders and drifted away
from the door. She sat down on the edge of a chair that
had a cigarette burn on the arm. The room was a
furnished-apartment living room with a lot of department store bric-à-brac spread around. Two floor lamps
burned. There were flounced pillows on the floor, a
French doll sprawled against the base of one lamp, and
a row of gaudy novels went across the mantel, above the
gas fire.

Dalmas said politely, swinging his hat: "It's about a
gun Dart Burwand used to own. It's showed up on a

case I'm working. I'm trying to trace it—from the time you had it."

Helen Dalton scratched the upper part of her arm. She had half-inch-long fingernails. She said curtly: "I don't have an idea what you're talking about."

Dalmas stared at her and leaned against the wall. His voice got on edge.

"Maybe you remember that you used to be married to Dart Burwand and that he got bumped off last April . . . Or is that too far back?"

The blonde bit one of her knuckles and said: "Smart guy, huh?"

"Not unless I have to be. But don't fall asleep from that last shot in the arm."

Helen Dalton sat up very straight, suddenly. All the vagueness went out of her expression. She spoke between tight lips.

"What's the howl about the gun?"

"It killed a guy, that's all," Dalmas said carelessly.

She stared at him. After a moment she said: "I was broke. I hocked it. I never got it out. I had a husband that made sixty bucks a week but didn't spend any of it on me. I never had a dime."

Dalmas nodded. "Remember the pawnshop where you left it?" he asked. "Or maybe you still have the ticket."

"No. It was on Main. The street's lined with them. And I don't have the ticket."

Dalmas said: "I was afraid of that."

He walked slowly across the room, looked at the titles of some of the books on the mantel. He went on and stood in front of a small, folding desk. There was a photo in a silver frame on the desk. Dalmas stared at it for some time. He turned slowly.

"It's too bad about the gun, Helen. A pretty important name was rubbed out with it this afternoon. The number was filed off the outside. If you hocked it, I'd figure some hood bought it from the hockshop guy, except that a hood wouldn't file a gun that way. He'd know there was another number inside. So it wasn't a hood—and the man it was found with wouldn't be likely to get a gun in a hock shop."

The blonde stood up slowly. Red spots burned in her cheeks. Her arms were rigid at her sides and her breath whispered. She said slowly, strainedly: "You can't maul me around, dick. I don't want any part of any police business—and I've got some good friends to take care of me. Better scram."

Dalmas looked back towards the frame on the desk. He said: "Johnny Sutro oughtn't to leave his mug around in a broad's apartment that way. Somebody might think he was cheating."

The blonde walked stiff-legged across the room and slammed the photo into the drawer of the desk. She slammed the drawer shut, and leaned her hips against the desk.

"You're all wet, shamus. That's not anybody called Sutro. Get on out, will you, for gawd's sake?"

Dalmas laughed unpleasantly. "I saw you at Sutro's house this afternoon. You were so drunk you don't remember."

The blonde made a movement as though she were going to jump at him. Then she stopped, rigid. A key turned in the room door. It opened and a man came in. He stood just inside the door and pushed it shut very slowly. His right hand was in the pocket of a light tweed overcoat. He was dark-skinned, high-shouldered, angular, with a sharp nose and chin.

Dalmas looked at him quietly and said: "Good evening, Councilman Sutro."

The man looked past Dalmas at the girl. He took no notice of Dalmas. The girl said shakily: "This guy says he's a dick. He's giving me a third about some gun he says I had. Throw him out, will you?"

Sutro said: "A dick, eh?"

He walked past Dalmas without looking at him. The

blonde backed away from him and fell into a chair. Her face got a pasty look and her eyes were scared. Sutro looked down at her for a moment, then turned around and took a small automatic out of his pocket. He held it loosely, pointed down at the floor.

He said: "I haven't a lot of time."

Dalmas said: "I was just going." He moved near the door. Sutro said sharply: "Let's have the story first."

Dalmas said: "Sure."

He moved lithely, without haste, and threw the door wide open. The gun jerked up in Sutro's hand. Dalmas said: "Don't be a sap. You're not starting anything here and you know it."

The two men stared at each other. After a moment or two Sutro put the gun back into his pocket and licked his thin lips. Dalmas said: "Miss Dalton had a gun once that killed a man—recently. But she hasn't had it for a long time. That's all I wanted to know."

Sutro nodded slowly. There was a peculiar expression in his eyes.

"Miss Dalton is a friend of my wife's. I wouldn't want her to be bothered," he said coldly.

"That's right. You wouldn't," Dalmas said "But a legitimate dick has a right to ask legitimate questions. I didn't break in here."

Sutro eyed him slowly: "Okey, but take it easy on my friends. I draw water in this town and I could hang a sign on you."

Dalmas nodded. He went quietly out of the door and shut it. He listened a moment. There was no sound inside that he could hear. He shrugged and went on down the hall, down three steps and across a small lobby that had no switchboard. Outside the apartment house he looked along the street. It was an apartment-house district and there were cars parked up and down the street. He went towards the lights of the taxi that was waiting for him.

Joey, the red-haired driver, was standing on the edge

of the curb in front of his hack. He was smoking a cigarette, staring across the street, apparently at a big, dark coupe that was parked with its left side to the curb. As Dalmas came up to him he threw his cigarette away and came to meet him.

He spoke quickly: "Listen, boss. I got a look at the guy in that Cad—"

Pale flame broke in bitter streaks from above the door of the coupe. A gun racketed between the buildings that faced each other across the street. Joey fell against Dalmas. The coupe jerked into sudden motion. Dalmas went down sidewise, on to one knee, with the driver clinging to him. He tried to reach his gun, couldn't make it. The coupe went around the corner with a squeal of rubber, and Joey fell down Dalmas' side and rolled over on his back on the sidewalk. He beat his hands up and down on the cement and a hoarse, anguished sound came from deep inside him.

Tires screeched again and Dalmas flung up to his feet, swept his hand to his left armpit. He relaxed as a small car skidded to a stop and Denny fell out of it, charged across the intervening space towards him.

Dalmas bent over the driver. Light from the lanterns beside the entrance to the apartment house showed blood on the front of Joey's whipcord jacket, blood that was seeping out through the material. Joey's eyes opened and shut like the eyes of a dying bird.

Denny said: "No use to follow that bus. Too fast."

"Get on a phone and call an ambulance," Dalmas said quickly. "The kid's got a bellyful . . . Then take a plant on the blonde."

The big man hurried back to his car, jumped into it and tore off around the corner. A window went open somewhere and a man yelled down. Some cars stopped.

Dalmas bent down over Joey and muttered: "Take it easy, oldtimer . . . Easy, boy . . . easy."

# 7

The homicide lieutenant's name was Weinkassel. He had thin, blond hair, icy blue eyes and a lot of pockmarks. He sat in a swivel chair with his feet on the edge of a pulled-out drawer and a telephone scooped close to his elbow. The room smelled of dust and cigar butts.

A man named Lonergan, a bulky dick with gray hair and a gray mustache, stood near an open window, looking out of it morosely.

Weinkassel chewed on a match, stared at Dalmas, who was across the desk from him. He said: "Better talk a bit. The hack driver can't. You've had luck in this town and you wouldn't want to run it into the ground."

Lonergan said: "He's hard. He won't talk." He didn't turn around when he said it.

"A little less of your crap would go farther, Lonnie," Weinkassel said in a dead voice.

Dalmas smiled faintly and rubbed the palm of his hand against the side of the desk. It made a squeaking sound.

"What would I talk about?" he asked. "It was dark and I didn't get a flash of the man behind the gun. The car was a Cadillac coupe, without lights. I've told you this already, Lieutenant."

"It don't listen," Weinkassel grumbled. "There's something screwy about it. You gotta have some kind of a hunch who it could be. It's a cinch the gun was for you."

Dalmas said: "Why? The hack driver was hit and I wasn't. Those lads get around a lot. One of them might be in wrong with some tough boys."

"Like you," Lonergan said. He went on staring out of the window.

Weinkassel frowned at Lonergan's back and said patiently: "The car was outside while you was still inside. The hack driver was outside. If the guy with the gun had wanted him, he didn't have to wait for you to come out."

Dalmas spread his hands and shrugged. "You boys think I know who it was?"

"Not exactly. We think you could give us some names to check on, though. Who'd you go to see in them apartments?"

Dalmas didn't say anything for a moment. Lonergan turned away from the window, sat on the end of the desk and swung his legs. There was a cynical grin on his flat face.

"Come through, baby," he said cheerfully.

Dalmas tilted his chair back and put his hands into his pockets. He stared at Weinkassel speculatively, ignored the gray-haired dick as though he didn't exist.

He said slowly: "I was there on business for a client. You can't make me talk about that."

Weinkassel shrugged and stared at him coldly. Then he took the chewed match out of his mouth, looked at the flattened end of it, tossed it away.

"I might have a hunch your business had something to do with the shootin'," he said grimly. "That way the hush-hush would be out. Wouldn't it?"

"Maybe," Dalmas said. "If that's the way it's going to work out. But I ought to have a chance to talk to my client."

Weinkassel said: "Oke. You can have till the morning. Then you put your papers on the desk, see."

Dalmas nodded and stood up. "Fair enough, Lieutenant."

"Hush-hush is all a shamus knows," Lonergan said roughly.

Dalmas nodded to Weinkassel and went out of the office. He walked down a bleak corridor and up steps to the lobby floor. Outside the City Hall he went down a long flight of concrete steps and across Spring Street to where a blue Packard roadster, not very new, was parked. He got into it and drove around the corner, then though the Second Street tunnel, dropped over a block and drove out west. He watched in the mirror as he drove.

At Alvarado he went into a drugstore and called his hotel. The clerk gave him a number to call. He called it and heard Denny's heavy voice at the other end of the line. Denny said urgently: "Where you been? I've got that broad out here at my place. She's drunk. Come on out and we'll get her to tell us what you want to know."

Dalmas stared out through the glass of the phone booth without seeing anything. After a pause he said slowly: "The blonde? How come?"

"It's a story, boy. Come on out and I'll give it to you. Fourteen-fifty-four South Livesay. Know where that is?"

"I've got a map. I'll find it," Dalmas said in the same tone.

Denny told him just how to find it, at some length. At the end of the explanation he said: "Make it fast. She's asleep now, but she might wake up and start yellin' murder."

Dalmas said: "Where you live it probably wouldn't matter much . . . I'll be right out, Denny."

He hung up and went out to his car. He got a pint bottle of bourbon out of the car pocket and took a long drink. Then he started up and drove towards Fox Hills. Twice on the way he stopped and sat still in the car, thinking. But each time he went on again.

## 8

The road turned off Pico into a scattered subdivision that spread itself out over rolling hills between two golf courses. It followed the edge of one of the golf courses, separated from it by a high wire fence. There were bungalows here and there dotted about the slopes. After a while the road dipped into a hollow and there was a single bungalow in the hollow, right across the street from the golf course.

Dalmas drove past it and parked under a giant eucalyptus that etched deep shadow on the moonlit surface of the road. He got out and walked back, turned up a cement path to the bungalow. It was wide and low and had cottage windows across the front. Bushes grew halfway up the screens. There was faint light inside and the sound of a radio, turned low, came through the open windows.

A shadow moved across the screens and the front door came open. Dalmas went into a living room built across the front of the house. One small bulb burned in a lamp and the luminous dial of the radio glowed. A little moonlight came into the room.

Denny had his coat off and his sleeves rolled up on his big arms.

He said: "The broad's still asleep. I'll wake her up when I've told you how I got her here."

Dalmas said: "Sure you weren't tailed?"

"Not a chance." Denny spread a big hand.

Dalmas sat down in a wicker chair in the corner, between the radio and the end of the line of windows. He put his hat on the floor, pulled out the bottle of bourbon and regarded it with a dissatisfied air.

"Buy us a real drink, Denny. I'm tired as hell. Didn't get any dinner."

Denny said: "I've got some Three-Star Martel. Be right up."

He went out of the room and light went on in the back part of the house. Dalmas put the bottle on the floor beside his hat and rubbed two fingers across his forehead. His head ached. After a little while the light went out in the back and Denny came back with two tall glasses.

The brandy tasted clean and hard. Denny sat down in another wicker chair. He looked very big and dark in the half-lit room. He began to talk slowly, in his gruff voice.

"It sounds goofy, but it worked. After the cops stopped milling around I parked in the alley and went in the back way. I knew which apartment the broad had but I hadn't seen her. I thought I'd make some kind of a stall and see how she was makin' out. I knocked on her door, but she wouldn't answer. I could hear her movin' around inside, and in a minute I could hear a telephone bein' dialed. I went back along the hall and tried the service door. It opened and I went in. It fastened with one of them screw bolts that get out of line and don't fasten when you think they do."

Dalmas nodded, said: "I get the idea, Denny."

The big man drank out of his glass and rubbed the edge of it up and down on his lower lip. He went on.

"She was phoning a guy named Gayn Donner. Know him?"

"I've heard of him," Dalmas said. "So she has that kind of connections."

"She was callin' him by name and she sounded mad," Denny said. "That's how I knew. Donner has that place on Mariposa Canyon Drive—the Mariposa Club. You hear his band over the air—Hank Munn and his boys."

Dalmas said: "I've heard it, Denny."

"Okey. When she hung up I went in on her. She looked snowed, weaved around funny, didn't seem to know much what was going on. I looked around and there was a photo of John Sutro, the Councilman, in a desk there. I used that for a stall. I said that Sutro wanted her to duck out for a while and that I was one of his boys and she was to come along. She fell for it. Screwy. She wanted some liquor. I said I had some in the car. She got her little hat and coat."

Dalmas said softly: "It was that easy, huh?"

"Yeah," Denny said. He finished his drink and put the glass somewhere. "I bottle-fed her in the car to keep her quiet and we came out here. She went to sleep and that's that. What do you figure? Tough downtown?"

"Tough enough," Dalmas said. "I didn't fool the boys much."

"Anything on the Walden kill?"

Dalmas shook his head slowly.

"I guess the Jap didn't get home yet, Denny."

"Want to talk to the broad?"

The radio was playing a waltz. Dalmas listened to it for a moment before he answered. Then he said in a tired voice: "I guess that's what I came out here for."

Denny got up and went out of the room. There was the sound of a door opening and muffled voices.

Dalmas took his gun out from under his arm and put it down in the chair beside his leg.

The blonde staggered a little too much as she came in. She stared around, giggled, made vague motions with her long hands. She blinked at Dalmas, stood swaying a moment, then slid down into the chair Denny had been sitting in. The big man kept near her and leaned against a library table that stood by the inside wall.

She said drunkenly: "My old pal the dick. Hey, hey, stranger! How about buyin' a lady a drink?"

Dalmas stared at her without expression. He said slowly: "Got any new ideas about that gun? You know, the one we were talking about when Johnny Sutro crashed in . . . The filed gun . . . The gun that killed Derek Walden."

Denny stiffened, then made a sudden motion towards his hip. Dalmas brought his Colt up and came to his feet with it. Denny looked at it and became still, relaxed. The girl had not moved at all, but the drunkenness dropped away from her like a dead leaf. Her face was suddenly tense and bitter.

Dalmas said evenly: "Keep the hands in sight, Denny, and everything'll be jake . . . Now suppose you two cheap crossers tell me what I'm here for."

The big man said thickly: "For gawd's sake! What's eatin' you? You scared me when you said 'Walden' to the girl."

Dalmas grinned. "That's all right, Denny. Maybe she never heard of him. Let's get this ironed out in a hurry. I have an idea I'm here for trouble."

"You're crazy as hell!" the big man snarled.

Dalmas moved the gun slightly. He put his back against the end wall of the room, leaned over and turned the radio off with his left hand. Then he spoke bitterly: "You sold out, Denny. That's easy. You're too big for a tail and I've spotted you following me around half a dozen times lately. When you horned in on the deal tonight I was pretty sure . . . And when you told me that funny story about how you got baby out here I was *damn* sure . . . Hell's sake, do you think a guy that's stayed alive as long as I have would believe that one? Come on, Denny, be a sport and tell me who you're working for . . . I might let you take a powder . . . Who you working for? Donner? Sutro? Or somebody I don't know? And why the plant out here in the woods?"

The girl shot to her feet suddenly and sprang at him. He threw her off with his free hand and she sprawled on the floor. She yelled: "Get him, you big punk? Get him!"

Denny didn't move. "Shut up, snow-bird!" Dalmas snapped. "Nobody's getting anybody. This is just a talk between friends. Get up on your feet and stop throwing curves!"

The blonde stood up slowly.

Denny's face had a stony, immovable look in the dimness. His voice came with a dull rasp. He said: "I sold out. It was lousy. Okey, that's that. I got fed up with watchin' a bunch of extra girls trying to pinch each other's lipstick . . . You can take a plug at me, if you feel like it."

He still didn't move. Dalmas nodded slowly and said again: "Who is it, Denny? Who you working for?"

Denny said: "I don't know. I call a number, get orders, and report that way. I get dough in the mail. I tried to break the twist here, but no luck ... I don't think you're on the spot and I don't know a damn thing about that shootin' in the street."

Dalmas stared at him. He said slowly: "You wouldn't be stalling—to keep me here—would you, Denny?"

The big man raised his head slowly. The room suddenly seemed to get very still. A car had stopped outside. The faint throbbing of its motor died.

A red spotlight hit the top of the screens.

It was blinding. Dalmas slid down on one knee, shifted his position sidewise very quickly, silently. Denny's harsh voice in the silence said: "Cops, for gawd's sake!"

The red light dissolved the wire mesh of the screens into a rosy glow, threw a great splash of vivid color on the oiled finish of the inside wall. The girl made a choked sound and her face was a red mask for an instant before she sank down out of the fan of light. Dalmas looked into the light, his head low behind the sill of the end window. The leaves of the bushes were black spearpoints in the red glare.

Steps sounded on the walk.

A harsh voice rasped: "Everybody out! Mitts in the air!"

There was a sound of movement inside the house. Dalmas swung his gun—uselessly. A switch clicked and a porch light went on. For a moment, before they dodged back, two men in blue police uniforms showed up in the cone of the porch light. One of them held a sub-machine gun and the other had a long Luger with a special magazine fitted to it.

There was a grating sound. Denny was at the door, opening the peep panel. A gun came up in his hand and crashed.

Something heavy clattered on the cement and a man swayed forward into the light, swayed back again. His hands were against his middle. A stiff-vizored cap fell down and rolled on the walk.

Dalmas hit the floor low down against the baseboard as the machine gun cut loose. He ground his face into the wood of the floor. The girl screamed behind him.

The chopper raked the room swiftly from end to end and the air filled with plaster and splinters. A wall mirror crashed down. A sharp stench of powder fought with the sour smell of the plaster dust. This seemed to go on for a very long time. Something fell across Dalmas' legs. He kept his eyes shut and his face pressed against the floor.

The stuttering and crashing stopped. The rain of plaster inside the walls kept on. A voice yelled: "How d'you like it, pals?"

Another voice far back snapped angrily: "Come on—let's go!"

Steps sounded again, and a dragging sound. More steps. The motor of the car roared into life. A door slammed heavily. Tires screeched on the gravel of the road and the song of the motor swelled and died swiftly.

Dalmas got up on his feet. His ears boomed and his nostrils were dry. He got his gun off the floor, unclipped a thin flash from an inside pocket, snapped it on. It probed weakly through the dusty air. The blonde lay on her back with her eyes wide open and her mouth twisted into a sort of grin. She was sobbing. Dalmas bent over her. There didn't seem to be a mark on her.

He went on down the room. He found his hat untouched beside the chair that had half the top shot off. The bottle of bourbon lay beside the hat. He picked them both up. The man with the chopper had raked the room waist-high, back and forth, without lowering it far enough. Dalmas went on farther, came to the door.

Denny was on his knees in front of the door. He was

swaying backwards and forwards and holding one of his hands in the other. Blood dribbled between his thick fingers.

Dalmas got the door open and went out. There was a smear of blood and a litter of shells on the walk. There was nobody in sight. He stood there with the blood beating in his face, like little hammers. The skin around his nose prickled.

He drank some whiskey out of the bottle and turned and went back into the house. Denny was up on his feet now. He had a handkerchief out and was tying it around his bloody hand. He looked dazed, drunk. He swayed on his feet. Dalmas put the beam of the flash on his face.

He said: "Hurt much?"

"No. Clipped on the hand," the big man said thickly. His fingers were clumsy on the handkerchief.

"The blonde's scared blind," Dalmas said. "It's your party, boy. Nice pals you have. They meant to get all three of us. You rattled them when you took a pot out of the peephole. I guess I owe you something for that, Denny . . . The gunner wasn't so good."

Denny said: "Where you goin'?"

"Where d'you think?"

Denny looked at him. "Sutro's your man," he said slowly. "I'm through—washed up. They can all go to hell."

Dalmas went through the door again, down the path to the street. He got into his car and drove away without lights. When he had turned corners and gone some distance he switched the lights on and got out and dusted himself off.

## 9

Black and silver curtains opened in an inverted V against a haze of cigarette and cigar smoke. The brasses of the dance band shot brief flashes of color through the haze. There was a smell of food and liquor and perfume and face powder. The dance floor was an empty splash of amber light and looked slightly larger than a screen star's bath mat.

Then the band started up and the lights went down, and a headwaiter came up the carpeted steps tapping a gold pencil against the satin stripe of his trousers. He had narrow, lifeless eyes and blond-white hair sleeked back off a bony forehead.

Dalmas said: "I'd like to see Mister Donner."

The headwaiter tapped his teeth with his gold pencil. "I'm afraid he's busy. What name?"

"Dalmas. Tell him I'm a special friend of Johnny Sutro's."

The headwaiter said: "I'll try."

He went across to a panel that had a row of buttons on it and a small one-piece phone. He took it off the hook and put it to his ear, staring at Dalmas across the cup with the impersonal stare of a stuffed animal.

Dalmas said: "I'll be in the lobby."

He went back through the curtains and prowled over to the Men's Room. Inside he got out the bottle of bourbon and drank what was left of it, tilting his head back and standing splay-legged in the middle of the tiled floor. A wizened Negro in a white jacket fluttered at him, said anxiously: "No drinkin' in here, boss."

Dalmas threw the empty bottle into a receptacle for towels. He took a clean towel off the glass shelf, wiped his lips with it, put a dime down on the edge of the basin and went out.

There was a space between an inner and outer door. He leaned against the outer door and took a small automatic about four inches long out of his vest pocket. He held it with three fingers against the inside of his hat and went on out, swinging the hat gently beside his body.

After a while a tall Filipino with silky black hair

came into the lobby and looked around. Dalmas went towards him. The headwaiter looked out through the curtains and nodded at the Filipino.

The Filipino spoke to Dalmas: "This way, boss."

They went down a long, quiet corridor. The sound of the dance band died away behind them. Some deserted green-topped tables showed through an open door. The corridor turned into another that was at right angles, and at the end of this one some light came out through a doorway.

The Filipino paused in midstride and made a graceful, complicated movement, at the end of which he had a big, black automatic in his hand. He prodded it politely into Dalmas' ribs.

"Got to frisk you, boss. House rules."

Dalmas stood still and held his arms out from his sides. The Filipino took Dalmas' Colt away from him and dropped it into his pocket. He patted the rest of Dalmas' pockets, stepped back and holstered his own cannon.

Dalmas lowered his arms and let his hat fall on the floor and the little automatic that had been inside the hat peered neatly at the Filipino's belly. The Filipino looked down at it with a shocked grin.

Dalmas said: "That was fun, spig. Let me do it."

He put his Colt back where it belonged, took the big automatic from under the Filipino's arm, slipped the magazine out of it and ejected the shell that was in the chamber. He gave the empty gun back to the Filipino.

"You can still use it for a sap. If you stay in front of me, your boss don't have to know that's all it's good for."

The Filipino licked his lips. Dalmas felt him for another gun, and they went on along the corridor, went in at the door that was partly open. The Filipino went first.

It was a big room with walls paneled in diagonal strips of wood. A yellow Chinese rug on the floor, plenty of good furniture, countersunk doors that told of soundproofing, and no windows. There were several gilt gratings high up and a built-in ventilator fan made a faint, soothing murmur. Four men were in the room. Nobody said anything.

Dalmas sat down on a leather divan and stared at Ricchio, the smooth boy who had walked him out of Walden's apartment. Ricchio was tied to a high-backed chair. His arms were pulled around behind it and fastened together at the wrists. His eyes were mad and his face was a welter of blood and bruises. He had been pistol whipped. The sandy-haired man, Noddy, who had been with him at the Kilmarnock sat on a sort of stool in the corner, smoking.

John Sutro was rocking slowly in a red leather rocker, staring down at the floor. He did not look up when Dalmas came into the room.

The fourth man sat behind a desk that looked as if it had cost a lot of money. He had soft brown hair parted in the middle and brushed back and down; thin lips and reddish-brown eyes that had hot lights in them. He watched Mallory while he sat down and looked around. Then he spoke, glancing at Ricchio.

"The punk got a little out of hand. We've been telling him about it. I guess you're not sorry."

Dalmas laughed shortly, without mirth. "All right as far as it goes, Donner. How about the other one? I don't see any marks on him."

"Noddy's all right. He worked under orders," Donner said evenly. He picked up a long-handled file and began to file one of his nails. "You and I have things to talk about. That's why you got in here. You look all right to me—if you don't try to cover too much ground with your private-dick racket."

Dalmas' eyes widened a little. He said: "I'm listening, Donner."

Sutro lifted his eyes and stared at the back of Donner's head. Donner went on talking in a smooth indifferent voice.

"I know all about the play at Derek Walden's place and I know about the shooting on Kenmore. If I'd thought Ricchio would go that crazy, I'd have stopped him before. As it is, I figure it's up to me to straighten things out ... And when we get through here Mister Ricchio will go downtown and speak his piece.

"Here's how it happened. Ricchio used to work for Walden when the Hollywood crowd went in for bodyguards. Walden bought his liquor in Ensenada—still does, for all I know—and brought it in himself. Nobody bothered him. Ricchio saw a chance to bring in some white goods under good cover. Walden caught him at it. He didn't want a scandal, so he just showed Ricchio the gate. Ricchio took advantage of that by trying to shake Walden down, on the theory that he wasn't clean enough to stand the working-over the Feds would give him. Walden didn't shake fast enough to suit Ricchio, so he went hog-wild and decided on a strong-arm play. You and your driver messed it up and Ricchio went gunning for you."

Donner put down his file and smiled. Dalmas shrugged and glanced at the Filipino, who was standing by the wall, at the end of the divan.

Dalmas said: "I don't have your organization, Donner, but I get around. I think that's a smooth story and it would have got by—with a little co-operation downtown. But it won't fit the facts as they are now."

Donner raised his eyebrows. Sutro began to swing the tip of his polished shoe up and down in front of his knee.

Dalmas said: "How does Mister Sutro fit into all this?"

Sutro stared at him and stopped rocking. He made a swift, impatient movement. Donner smiled "He's a friend of Walden's. Walden talked to him a little and Sutro knows Ricchio worked for me. But being a councilman he didn't want to tell Walden everything he knew."

Dalmas said grimly: "I'll tell you what's wrong with your story, Donner. There's not enough fear in it. Walden was too scared to help me even when I was working for him . . . And this afternoon somebody was so scared of him that he got shot."

Donner leaned forward and his eyes got small and tight. His hands balled into fists on the desk before him.

"Walden is—dead?" he almost whispered.

Dalmas nodded. "Shot in the right temple . . . with a thirty-two. It looks like suicide. It isn't."

Sutro put his hand up quickly and covered his face. The sandy-haired man got rigid on his stool in the corner.

Dalmas said: "Want to hear a good honest guess, Donner? . . . We'll call it a guess . . . Walden was in the dope-smuggling racket himself—and not all by his lonesome. But after Repeal he wanted to quit. The coast guards wouldn't have to spend so much time watching liquor ships, and dope-smuggling up the coast wasn't going to be gravy any more. And Walden got sweet on a gal that had good eyes and could add up to ten. So he wanted to walk out on the dope racket."

Donner moistened his lips and said: "What dope racket?"

Dalmas eyed him. "You wouldn't know about anything like that, would you, Donner? Hell, no, that's something for the bad boys to play with. And the bad boys didn't like the idea of Walden quitting that way. He was drinking too much—and he might start to broadcast to his girl friend. They wanted him to quit the way he did—on the receiving end of a gun."

Donner turned his head slowly and stared at the bound man on the high-backed chair. He said very softly: "Ricchio."

Then he got up and walked around his desk. Sutro

took his hand down from his face and watched with his
lips shaking.

Donner stood in front of Ricchio. He put his hand
out against Ricchio's head and jarred it back against the
chair. Ricchio moaned. Donner smiled down at him.

"I must be slowing up. *You* killed Walden, you
bastard! You went back and croaked him. You forgot
to tell us about that part, baby."

Ricchio opened his mouth and spit a stream of blood
against Donner's hand and wrist. Donner's face twitched
and he stepped back and away, holding the hand straight
out in front of him. He took out a handkerchief and
wiped it off carefully, dropped the handkerchief on the
floor.

"Lend me your gun, Noddy," he said quietly, going
towards the sandy-haired man.

Sutro jerked and his mouth fell open. His eyes
looked sick. The tall Filipino flicked his empty automatic into his hand as if he had forgotten it was empty.
Noddy took a blunt revolver from under his right arm,
held it out to Donner.

Donner took it from him and went back to Ricchio.
He raised the gun.

Dalmas said: Ricchio didn't kill Walden."

The Filipino took a quick step forward and slashed
at him with his big automatic. The gun hit Dalmas on
the point of the shoulder, and a wave of pain billowed
down his arm. He rolled away and snapped his Colt
into his hand. The Filipino swung at him again, missed.

Dalmas slid to his feet, side-stepped and laid the
barrel of the Colt along the side of the Filipino's head,
with all his strength. The Filipino grunted, sat down on
the floor, and the whites showed all around his eyes. He
fell over slowly, clawing at the divan.

There was no expression on Donner's face and he
held his blunt revolver perfectly still. His long upper lip
was beaded with sweat.

Dalmas said: "Ricchio didn't kill Walden. Walden

was killed with a filed gun and the gun was planted in his hand. Ricchio wouldn't go within a block of a filed gun."

Sutro's face was ghastly. The sandy-haired man had got down off his stool and stood with his right hand swinging at his side.

"Tell me more," Donner said evenly.

"The filed gun traces to a broad named Helen Dalton or Burwand," Dalmas said. "It was her gun. She told me that she hocked it long ago. I didn't believe her. She's a good friend of Sutro's and Sutro was so bothered by my going to see her that he pulled a gat on me himself. Why do you suppose Sutro was bothered, Donner, and how do you suppose he knew I was likely to go see the broad?"

Donner said: "Go ahead and tell me." He looked at Sutro very quietly.

Dalmas took a step closer to Donner and held his Colt down at his side, not threateningly.

"I'll tell you how and why. I've been tailed ever since I started to work for Walden—tailed by a clumsy ox of a studio dick I could spot a mile off. He was bought, Donner. The guy that killed Walden bought him. He figured the studio dick had a chance to get next to me, and I let him do just that—to give him rope and spot his game. His boss was Sutro. Sutro killed Walden—with his own hand. It was that kind of a job. An amateur job—a smart-aleck kill. The thing that made it smart was the thing that gave it away—the suicide plant, with a filed gun that the killer thought couldn't be traced because he didn't know most guns have numbers inside."

Donner swung the blunt revolver until it pointed midway between the sandy-haired man and Sutro. He didn't say anything. His eyes were thoughtful and interested.

Dalmas shifted his weight a little, on to the balls of

his feet. The Filipino on the floor put a hand along the divan and his nails scratched on the leather.

"There's more of it, Donner, but what the hell! Sutro was Walden's pal, and he could get close to him, close enough to stick a gun to his head and let go. A shot wouldn't be heard on the penthouse floor of the Kilmarnock, one little shot from a thirty-two. So Sutro put the gun in Walden's hand and went on his way. But he forgot that Walden was left-handed and he didn't know the gun could be traced. When it was—and his bought man wised him up—and I tapped the girl—he hired himself a chopper squad and angled all three of us out to a house in Palms to button our mouths for good ... Only the chopper squad, like everything else in this play, didn't do its stuff so good."

Donner nodded slowly. He looked at a spot in the middle of Sutro's stomach and lined his gun on it.

"Tell us about it, Johnny," he said softly. "Tell us how you got clever in your old age—"

The sandy-haired man moved suddenly. He dodged down behind the desk and as he went down his right hand swept for his other gun. It roared from behind the desk. The bullet came through the kneehole and pinged into the wall with a sound of striking metal behind the paneling.

Dalmas jerked his Colt and fired twice into the desk. A few splinters flew. The sandy-haired man yelled behind the desk and came up fast with his gun flaming in his hand. Donner staggered. His gun spoke twice, very quickly. The sandy-haired man yelled again, and blood jumped straight out from one of his cheeks. He went down behind the desk and stayed quiet.

Donner backed until he touched the wall. Sutro stood up and put his hands in front of his stomach and tried to scream.

Donner said: "Okey, Johnny. Your turn."

Then Donner coughed suddenly and slid down the wall with a dry rustle of cloth. He bent forward and dropped his gun and put his hands on the floor and went on coughing. His face got gray.

Sutro stood rigid, his hands in front of his stomach, and bent back at the wrists, the fingers curved clawlike. There was no light behind his eyes. They were dead eyes. After a moment his knees buckled and he fell down on the floor on his back.

Donner went on coughing quietly.

Dalmas crossed swiftly to the door of the room, listened at it, opened it and looked out. He shut it again quickly.

"Soundproof—and how!" he muttered.

He went back to the desk and lifted the telephone off its prongs. He put his Colt down and dialed, waited, said into the phone: "Captain Cathcart . . . Got to talk to him . . . Sure, it's important . . . very important."

He waited, drumming on the desk, staring hard-eyed around the room. He jerked a little as a sleepy voice came over the wire.

"Dalmas, Chief. I'm at the Casa Mariposa, in Gayn Donner's private office. There's been a little trouble, but nobody hurt bad . . . I've got Derek Walden's killer for you . . . Johnny Sutro did it . . . Yeah, the councilman . . . Make it fast, Chief . . . I wouldn't want to get in a fight with the help, you know. . . ."

He hung up and picked his Colt off the top of the desk, held it on the flat of his hand and stared across at Sutro.

"Get off the floor, Johnny," he said wearily. "Get up and tell a poor dumb dick how to cover this one up—smart guy!"

## 10

The light above the big oak table at Headquarters was too bright. Dalmas ran a finger along the wood, looked at it, wiped it off on his sleeve. He cupped his chin in his lean hands and stared at the wall above the roll-top desk that was beyond the table. He was alone in the room.

The loudspeaker on the wall droned: "Calling Car 71W in 72's district . . . at Third and Berendo . . . at the drugstore . . . meet a man . . ."

The door opened and Captain Cathcart came in, shut the door carefully behind him. He was a big, battered man with a wide, moist face, a strained mustache, gnarled hands.

He sat down between the oak table and the roll-top desk and fingered a cold pipe that lay in the ashtray.

Dalmas raised his head from between his hands. Cathcart said: "Sutro's dead."

Dalmas stared, said nothing.

"His wife did it. He wanted to stop by his house a minute. The boys watched him good but they didn't watch her. She slipped him the dose before they could move."

Cathcart opened and shut his mouth twice. He had strong, dirty teeth.

"She never said a damn word. Brought a little gun around from behind her and fed him three slugs. One, two, three. Win, place, show. Just like that. Then she turned the gun around in her hand as nice as you could think of and handed it to the boys . . . What in hell she do that for?"

Dalmas said: "Get a confession?"

Cathcart stared at him and put the cold pipe in his mouth. He sucked on it noisily. "From him? Yeah— not on paper, though . . . What you suppose she done that for?"

"She knew about the blonde," Dalmas said. "She thought it was her last chance. Maybe she knew about his rackets."

The captain nodded slowly. "Sure," he said. "That's it. She figured it was her last chance. And why shouldn't she bop the bastard? If the D.A.'s smart, he'll let her take a manslaughter plea. That'd be about fifteen months at Tehachapi. A rest cure."

Dalmas moved in his chair. He frowned.

Cathcart went on: "It's a break for all of us. No dirt your way, no dirt on the administration. If she hadn't done it, it would have been a kick in the pants all around. She ought to get a pension."

"She ought to get a contract from Eclipse Films," Dalmas said. "When I got to Sutro I figured I was licked on the publicity angle. I might have gunned Sutro myself—if he hadn't been so yellow—and if he hadn't been a councilman."

"Nix on that, baby. Leave that stuff to the law," Cathcart growled. "Here's how it looks. I don't figure we can get Walden on the book as a suicide. The filed gun is against it and we got to wait for the autopsy and the gun-shark's report. And a paraffin test of the hand ought to show he didn't fire the gun at all. On the other hand, the case is closed on Sutro and what has to come out ought not to hurt too bad. Am I right?"

Dalmas took out a cigarette and rolled it between his fingers. He lit it slowly and waved the match until it went out.

"Walden was no lily," he said. "It's the dope angle that would raise hell—but that's cold. I guess we're jake, except for a few loose ends."

"Hell with the loose ends," Cathcart grinned. "Nobody's getting away with any fix that I can see. That sidekick of yours, Denny, will fade in a hurry and if I ever get my paws on the Dalton frail, I'll send her to Mendocino for the cure. We might get something on Donner—after the hospital gets through with him. We've got to put the rap on those hoods, for the stick-up and the taxi driver, whichever of 'em did that, but they won't talk. They still got a future to think about, and the taxi driver ain't so bad hurt. That leaves the chopper squad." Cathcart yawned. "Those boys must be from Frisco. We don't run to choppers around here much."

Dalmas sagged in his chair. "You wouldn't have a drink, would you, Chief?" he said dully.

Cathcart stared at him. "There's just one thing," he said grimly. "I want you to stay told about that. It was okey for you to break that gun—if you didn't spoil the prints. And I guess it was okey for you not to tell me, seein' the jam you were in. But I'll be damned if it's okey for you to beat our time by chiselin' on our own records."

Dalmas smiled thoughtfully at him. "You're right all the way, Chief," he said humbly. "It was the job—and that's all a guy can say."

Cathcart rubbed his cheeks vigorously. His frown went away and he grinned. Then he bent over and pulled out a drawer and brought up a quart bottle of rye. He put it on the desk and pressed a buzzer. A very large uniformed torso came part way into the room.

"Hey, Tiny!" Cathcart boomed. "Loan me that corkscrew you swiped out of my desk." The torso disappeared and came back.

"What'll we drink to?" the captain asked a couple of minutes later.

Dalmas said: "Let's just drink."

# GUNS
# AT CYRANO'S

TED CARMADY liked the rain; liked the feel of it, the sound of it, the smell of it. He got out of his LaSalle coupe and stood for a while by the side entrance to the Carondelet, the high collar of his blue suede ulster tickling his ears, his hands in his pockets and a limp cigarette sputtering between his lips. Then he went in past the barbershop and the drugstore and the perfume shop with its rows of delicately lighted bottles, ranged like the ensemble in the finale of a Broadway musical.

He rounded a gold-veined pillar and got into an elevator with a cushioned floor.

" 'Lo Albert. A swell rain. Nine."

The slim tired-looking kid in pale blue and silver held a white-goved hand against the closing doors, said: "Jeeze, you think I don't know your floor, Mister Carmady?"

He shot the car up to nine without looking at his signal light, whooshed the doors open, then leaned suddenly against the cage and closed his eyes.

Carmady stopped on his way out, flicked a sharp glance from bright brown eyes. "What's the matter, Albert? Sick?"

The boy worked a pale smile on his face. "I'm workin' double shift. Corky's sick. He's got boils. I guess maybe I didn't eat enough."

The tall, brown-eyed man fished a crumpled five-spot out of his pocket, snapped it under the boy's nose. The boy's eyes bulged. He heaved upright.

"Jeeze, Mister Carmady. I didn't mean—"

"Skip it, Albert. What's a fin between pals? Eat some extra meals on me."

He got out of the car and started along the corridor. Softly, under his breath, he said: "Sucker . . . "

The running man almost knocked him off his feet. He rounded the turn fast, lurched past Carmady's shoulder, ran for the elevator.

"Down!" He slammed through the closing doors.

Carmady saw a white set face under a pulled-down hat that was wet with rain; two empty black eyes set very close. Eyes in which there was a peculiar stare he had seen before. A load of dope.

The car dropped like lead. Carmady looked at the place where it had been for a long moment, then he went on down the corrdior and around the turn.

He saw the girl lying half in and half out of the open door of 914.

She lay on her side, in a sheen of steel-gray lounging pajamas, her cheek pressed into the nap of the hall carpet, her head a mass of thick corn-blond hair, waved with glassy precision. Not a hair looked out of place. She was young, very pretty, and she didn't look dead.

Carmady slid down beside her, touched her cheek. It was warm. He lifted the hair softly away from her head and saw the bruise.

"Sapped." His lips pressed back against his teeth.

He picked her up in his arms, carried her through a short hallway to the living room of a suite, put her down on a big velour davenport in front of some gas logs.

She lay motionless, her eyes shut, her face bluish behind the make-up. He shut the outer door and looked through the apartment, then went back to the hallway and picked up something that gleamed white against the baseboard. It was a bone-handled .22 automatic, sevenshot. He sniffed it, dropped it into his pocket and went back to the girl.

He took a big hammered-silver flask out of his inside breast pocket and unscrewed the top, opened her mouth with his fingers and poured whiskey against her small white teeth. She gagged and her head jerked out of his hand. Her eyes opened. They were deep blue, with a tint of purple. Light came into them and the light was brittle.

He lit a cigarette and stood looking down at her. She moved a little more. After a while she whispered: "I like your whiskey. Could I have a little more?"

He got a glass from the bathroom, poured whiskey into it. She sat up very slowly, touched her head, groaned. Then she took the glass out of his hand and put the liquor down with a practised flip of the wrist.

"I still like it," she said. "Who are you?"

She had a deep soft voice. He liked the sound of it. He said: "Ted Carmady. I live down the hall in 937."

"I—I got a dizzy spell, I guess."

"Uh-huh. You got sapped, angel." His bright eyes looked at her probingly. There was a smile tucked to the corners of his lips.

Her eyes got wider. A glaze came over them, the glaze of a protective enamel.

He said: "I saw the guy. He was snowed to the hairline. And here's your gun."

He took it out of his pocket, held it on the flat of his hand.

"I suppose that makes me think up a bedtime story," the girl said slowly.

"Not for me. If you're in a jam, I might help you. It all depends."

"Depends on what?" Her voice was colder, sharper.

"On what the racket is," he said softly. He broke the magazine from the small gun, glanced at the top cartridge. "Copper-nickel, eh? You know your ammunition, angel."

"Do you have to call me angel?"

"I don't know your name."

He grinned at her, then walked over to a desk in front of the windows, put the gun down on it. There was a leather photo frame on the desk, with two photos side by side. He looked at them casually at first, then his gaze tightened. A handsome dark woman and a thin blondish cold-eyed man whose high stiff collar, large knotted tie and narrow lapels dated the photo back many years. He stared at the man.

The girl was talking behind him. "I'm Jean Adrian. I do a number at Cyrano's, in the floor show."

Carmady still stared at the photo. "I know Benny Cyrano pretty well," he said absently. "These your parents?"

He turned and looked at her. She lifted her head slowly. Something that might have been fear showed in her deep blue eyes.

"Yes. They've been dead for years," she said dully. "Next question?"

He went quickly back to the davenport and stood in front of her. "Okey," he said thinly. "I'm nosey. So what? This is my town. My dad used to run it. Old Marcus Carmady, the People's Friend; this is my hotel. I own a piece of it. That snowed-up hoodlum looked like a life-taker to me. Why wouldn't I want to help out?"

The blond girl stared at him lazily. "I still like your whiskey," she said. "Could I—"

"Take it from the neck, angel. You get it down faster," he grunted.

She stood up suddenly and her face got a little white. "You talk to me as if I was a crook," she snapped. "Here it is, if you have to know. A boy friend of mine has been getting threats. He's a fighter, and they want him to drop a fight. Now they're trying to get at him through me. Does that satisfy you a little?"

Carmady picked his hat off a chair, took the cigarette end out of his mouth and rubbed it out in a tray. He nodded quietly, said in a changed voice: "I beg your pardon." He started towards the door.

The giggle came when he was halfway there. The girl said behind him softly: "You have a nasty temper. And you've forgotten your flask."

He went back and picked the flask up. Then he bent suddenly, put a hand under the girl's chin and kissed her on the lips.

"To hell with you, angel. I like you," he said softly.

He went back to the hallway and out. The girl touched her lips with one finger, rubbed it slowly back and forth. There was a shy smile on her face.

## 2

Tony Acosta, the bell captain, was slim and dark and slight as a girl, with small delicate hands and velvety eyes and a hard little mouth. He stood in the doorway and said: "Seventh row was the best I could get, Mister Carmady. This Deacon Werra ain't bad and Duke Targo's the next light heavy champ."

Carmady said: "Come in and have a drink, Tony." He went over to the window, stood looking out at the rain. "If they buy it for him," he added over his shoulder.

"Well—just a short one, Mister Carmady."

The dark boy mixed a highball carefully at a tray on an imitation Sheraton desk. He held the bottle against the light and gauged his drink carefully, tinkled ice gently with a long spoon, sipped, smiled, showing small white teeth.

"Targo's a lu, Mister Carmady. He's fast, clever, got

a sock in both mitts, plenty guts, don't ever take a step back."

"He has to hold up the bums they feed him," Carmady drawled.

"Well, they ain't fed him no lion meat yet," Tony said.

The rain beat against the glass. The thick drops flattened out and washed down the pane in tiny waves.

Carmady said: "He's a bum. A bum with color and looks, but still a bum."

Tony sighed deeply. "I wisht I was goin'. It's my night off, too."

Carmady turned slowly and went over to the desk, mixed a drink. Two dusky spots showed in his cheeks and his voice was tired, drawling.

"So that's it. What's stopping you?"

"I got a headache."

"You're broke again," Carmady almost snarled.

The dark boy looked sidewise under his long lashes, said nothing.

Carmady clenched his left hand, unclenched it slowly. His eyes were sullen.

"Just ask Carmady," he sighed. "Good old Carmady. He leaks dough. He's soft. Just ask Carmady. Okey, Tony, take the ducat back and get a pair together."

He reached into his pocket, held a bill out. The dark boy looked hurt.

"Jeeeze, Mister Carmady, I wouldn't have you think—"

"Skip it! What's a fight ticket between pals? Get a couple and take your girl. To hell with this Targo."

Tony Acosta took the bill. He watched the older man carefully for a moment. Then his voice was very softy, saying: "I'd rather go with you, Mister Carmady. Targo knocks them over, and not only in the ring. He's got a peachy blonde right on this floor, Miss Adrian, in 914."

Carmady stiffened. He put his glass down slowly, turned it on the top of the desk. His voice got a little hoarse.

"He's still a bum, Tony. Okey, I'll meet you for dinner, in front of your hotel at seven."

"Jeeze, that's swell, Mister Carmady."

Tony Acosta went out softly, closed the outer door without a sound.

Carmady stood by the desk, his fingertips stroking the top of it, his eyes on the floor. He stood like that for a long time.

"Carmady, the All-American sucker," he said grimly, out loud. "A guy that plays with the help and carries the torch for stray broads. Yeah."

He finished his drink, looked at his wrist watch, put on his hat and the blue suede raincoat, went out. Down the corridor in front of 914 he stopped, lifted his hand to knock, then dropped it without touching the door.

He went slowly on to the elevators and rode down to the street and his car.

The *Tribune* office was at Fourth and Spring. Carmady parked around the corner, went in at the employees' entrance and rode to the fourth floor in a rickety elevator operated by an old man with a dead cigar in his mouth and a rolled magazine which he held six inches from his nose while he ran the elevator.

On the fourth floor big double doors were lettered City Room. Another old man sat outside them at a small desk with a call box.

Carmady tapped on the desk, said: "Adams. Carmady calling."

The old man made noises into the box, released a key, pointed with his chin.

Carmady went through the doors, past a horseshoe copy desk, then past a row of small desks at which typewriters were being banged. At the far end a lanky red-haired man was doing nothing with his feet on a pulled-out drawer, the back of his neck on the back of a dangerously tilted swivel chair and a big pipe in his mouth pointed straight at the ceiling.

When Carmady stood beside him he moved his eyes down without moving any other part of his body and said around the pipe: "Greetings, Carmady. How's the idle rich?"

Carmady said: "How's a glance at your clips on a guy named Courtway? State Senator John Myerson Courtway, to be precise."

Adams put his feet on the floor. He raised himself erect by pulling on the edge of his desk. He brought his pipe down level, took it out of his mouth and spit into a wastebasket. He said: "That old icicle? When was he ever news? Sure." He stood up wearily, added: "Come along, Uncle," and started along the end of the room.

They went along another row of desks, past a fat girl in smudged make-up who was typing and laughing at what she was writing.

They went through a door into a big room that was mostly six-foot tiers of filing cases with an occasional alcove in which there was a small table and a chair.

Adams prowled the filing cases, jerked one out and set a folder on a table.

"Park yourself. What's the graft?"

Carmady leaned on the table on an elbow, scuffed through a thick wad of cuttings. They were monotonous, political in nature, not front page. Senator Courtway said this and that on this and that matter of public interest, addressed this and that meeting, went or returned from this and that place. It all seemed very dull.

He looked at a few halftone cuts of a thin, white-haired man with a blank, composed face, deep set dark eyes in which there was no light or warmth. After a while he said: "Got a print I could sneeze? A real one, I mean."

Adams sighed, stretched himself, disappeared down

the line of file walls. He came back with a shiny black
and white photograph, tossed it down on the table.

"You can keep it," he said. "We got dozens. The guy
lives forever. Shall I have it autographed for you?"

Carmady looked at the photo with narrow eyes, for a
long time. "It's right," he said slowly. "Was Courtway
ever married?"

"Not since I left off my diapers," Adams growled.
"Probably not ever. Say, what'n hell's the mystery?"

Carmady smiled slowly at him. He reached his flask
out, set it on the table beside the folder. Adams' face
brightened swiftly and his long arm reached.

"Then he never had a kid," Carmady said.

Adams leered over the flask. "Well—not for publication, I guess. If I'm any judge of a mug, not at all." He
drank deeply, wiped his lips, drank again.

"And that," Carmady said, "is very funny indeed.
Have three more drinks—and forget you ever saw me."

## 3

The fat man put his face close to Carmady's face. He
said with a wheeze: "You think it's fixed, neighbor?"

"Yeah. For Werra."

"How much says so?"

"Count your poke."

"I got five yards that want to grow."

"Take it," Carmady said tonelessly, and kept on
looking at the back of a corn-blond head in a ringside
seat. A white wrap with white fur was below the glassi-
ly waved hair. He couldn't see the face. He didn't have
to.

The fat man blinked his eyes and got a thick wallet
carefully out of a pocket inside his vest. He held it on
the edge of his knee, counted out ten fifty-dollar bills,
rolled them up, edged the wallet back against his ribs.

"You're on, sucker," he wheezed. "Let's see your dough."

Carmady brought his eyes back, reached out a flat pack of new hundreds, riffled them. He slipped five from under the printed band, held them out.

"Boy, this is from home," the fat man said. He put his face close to Carmady's face again. "I'm Skeets O'Neal. No little powders, huh?"

Carmady smiled very slowly and pushed his money into the fat man's hand. "You hold it, Skeets. I'm Carmady. Old Marcus Carmady's son. I can shoot faster than you can run—and fix it afterwards."

The fat man took a long hard breath and leaned back in his seat. Tony Acosta stared soft-eyed at the money in the fat man's pudgy tight hand. He licked his lips and turned a small embarrassed smile on Carmady.

"Gee, that's lost dough, Mister Carmady," he whispered. "Unless—unless you got something inside."

"Enough to be worth a five-yard plunge," Carmady growled.

The buzzer sounded for the sixth.

The first five had been anybody's fight. The big blond boy, Duke Targo, wasn't trying. The dark one, Deacon Werra, a powerful, loose-limbed Polack with bad teeth and only two cauliflower ears, had the physique but didn't know anything but rough clinching and a giant swing that started in the basement and never connected. He had been good enough to hold Targo off so far. The fans razzed Targo a good deal.

When the stool swung back out of the ring Targo hitched at his black and silver trunks, smiled with a small tight smile at the girl in the white wrap. He was very good-looking, without a mark on him. There was blood on his left shoulder from Werra's nose.

The bell rang and Werra charged across the ring, slid off Targo's shoulder, got a left hook in. Targo got more of the hook than was in it. He piled back into the ropes, bounced out, clinched.

Carmady smiled quietly in the darkness.

The referee broke them easily. Targo broke clean, Werra tried for an uppercut and missed. They sparred for a minute. There was waltz music from the gallery. Then Werra started a swing from his shoetops. Targo seemed to wait for it, to wait for it to hit him. There was a queer strained smile on his face. The girl in the white wrap stood up suddenly.

Werra's swing grazed Targo's jaw. It barely staggered him. Targo lashed a long right that caught Werra over the eye. A left hook smashed Werra's jaw, then a right cross almost to the same spot.

The dark boy went down on his hands and knees, slipped slowly all the way to the floor, lay with both his gloves under him. There were catcalls as he was counted out.

The fat man struggled to his feet, grinning hugely. He said: "How you like it, pal? Still think it was a set piece?"

"It came unstuck," Carmady said in a voice as toneless as a police radio.

The fat man said: "So long, pal. Come around lots." He kicked Carmady's ankle climbing over him.

Carmady sat motionless, watched the auditorium empty. The fighters and their handlers had gone down the stairs under the ring. The girl in the white wrap had disappeared in the crowd. The lights went out and the barnlike structure looked cheap, sordid.

Tony Acosta fidgeted, watching a man in striped overalls picking up papers between the seats.

Carmady stood up suddenly, said: "I'm going to talk to that bum, Tony. Wait outside in the car for me."

He went swiftly up the slope to the lobby, through the remnants of the gallery crowd to a gray door marked "No Admittance." He went through that and down a ramp to another door marked the same way. A special cop in faded and unbuttoned khaki stood in front of it, with a bottle of beer in one hand and a hamburger in the other.

Carmady flashed a police card and the cop lurched out of the way without looking at the card. He hiccoughed peacefully as Carmady went through the door, then along a narrow passage with numbered doors lining it. There was noise behind the doors. The fourth door on the left had a scribbled card with the name "Duke Targo" fastened to the panel by a thumbtack.

Carmady opened it into the heavy sound of a shower going, out of sight.

In a narrow and utterly bare room a man in a white sweater was sitting on the end of a rubbing table that had clothes scattered on it. Carmady recognized him as Targo's chief second.

He said: "Where's the Duke?"

The sweatered man jerked a thumb towards the shower noise. Then a man came around the door and lurched very close to Carmady. He was tall and had curly brown hair with hard gray color in it. He had a big drink in his hand. His face had the flat glitter of extreme drunkenness. His hair was damp, his eyes bloodshot. His lips curled and uncurled in rapid smiles without meaning. He said thickly: "Scramola, umpchay."

Carmady shut the door calmly and leaned against it and started to get his cigarette case from his vest pocket, inside his open blue raincoat. He didn't look at the curly-haired man at all.

The curly-haired man lunged his free right hand up suddenly, snapped it under his coat, out again. A blue steel gun shone dully against his light suit. The glass in his left hand slopped liquor.

"None of that!" he snarled.

Carmady brought the cigarette case out very slowly, showed it in his hand, opened it and put a cigarette between his lips. The blue gun was very close to him, not very steady. The hand holding the glass shook in a sort of jerky rhythm.

Carmady said loosely: "You *ought* to be looking for trouble."

The sweatered man got off the rubbing table. Then he stood very still and looked at the gun. The curly-haired man said: "We like trouble. Frisk him, Mike."

The sweatered man said: "I don't want any part of it, Shenvair. For Pete's sake, take it easy. You're lit like a ferry boat."

Carmady said: "It's okey to frisk me. I'm not rodded."

"Nix," the sweatered man said. "This guy is the Duke's bodyguard. Deal me out."

The curly-haired man said: "Sure, I'm drunk," and giggled.

"You're a friend of the Duke?" the sweatered man asked.

"I've got some information for him," Carmady said.

"About what?"

Carmady didn't say anything. "Okey," the sweatered man said. He shrugged bitterly.

"Know what, Mike?" the curly-haired man said suddenly and violently. "I think this Sonofabitch wants my job. Hell, yes." He punched Carmady with the muzzle of the gun. "You ain't a shamus, are you, mister?"

"Maybe," Carmady said: "And keep your iron next your own belly."

The curly-haired man turned his head a little and grinned back over his shoulder.

"What d'you know about that, Mike? He's a shamus. Sure he wants my job. Sure he does."

"Put the heater up, you fool," the sweatered man said disgustedly.

The curly-haired man turned a little more. "I'm his protection, ain't I?" he complained.

Carmady knocked the gun aside almost casually, with the hand that held his cigarette case. The curly-haired man snapped his head around again. Carmady slid close to him, sank a stiff punch in his stomach,

holding the gun away with his forearm. The curly-
haired man gagged, sprayed liquor down the front of
Carmady's raincoat. His glass shattered on the floor.
The blue gun left his hand and went over in a corner.
The sweatered man went after it.

The noise of the shower had stopped unnoticed and
the blond fighter came out toweling himself vigorously.
He stared open-mouthed at the tableau.

Carmady said: "I don't need this any more."

He heaved the curly-haired man away from him and
laced his jaw with a hard right as he went back. The
curly-haired man staggered across the room, hit the
wall, slid down it and sat on the floor.

The sweatered man snatched the gun up and stood
rigid, watching Carmady.

Carmady got out a handkerchief and wiped the front
of his coat, while Targo shut his large well-shaped
mouth slowly and began to move the towel back and
forth across his chest. After a moment he said: "Just
who the hell may you be?"

Carmady said: "I used to be a private dick. Carmady's the name. I think you need help."

Targo's face got a little redder than the shower had
left it. "Why?"

"I heard you were supposed to throw it, and I think
you tried to. But Werra was too lousy. You couldn't
help yourself. That means you're in a jam."

Targo said very slowly: "People get their teeth kicked
in for saying things like that."

The room was very still for a moment. The drunk sat
up on the floor and blinked, tried to get his feet under
him, and gave it up.

Carmady added quietly: "Benny Cyrano is a friend
of mine. He's your backer, isn't he?"

The sweatered man laughed harshly. Then he broke
the gun and slid the shells out of it, dropped the gun on
the floor. He went to the door, went out, slammed the
door shut.

Targo looked at the shut door, looked back at Carmady. He said very slowly: "What did you hear?"

"Your friend Jean Adrian lives in my hotel, on my floor. She got sapped by a hood this afternoon. I happened by and saw the hood running away, picked her up. She told me a little of what it was all about."

Targo had put on his underwear and socks and shoes. He reached into a locker for a black satin shirt, put that on. He said: "She didn't tell me."

"She wouldn't—before the fight."

Targo nodded slightly. Then he said: "If you know Benny, you may be all right. I've been getting threats. Maybe it's a lot of birdseed and maybe it's some Spring Street punter's idea of how to make himself a little easy dough. I fought my fight the way I wanted to. Now you can take the air, mister."

He put on high-waisted black trousers and knotted a white tie on his black shirt. He got a white serge coat trimmed with black braid out of the locker, put that on. A black and white handkerchief flared from the pocket in three points.

Carmady stared at the clothes, moved a little towards the door and looked down at the drunk.

"Okey," he said. "I see you've got a bodyguard. It was just an idea I had. Excuse it, please."

He went out, closed the door gently, and went back up the ramp to the lobby, out to the street. He walked through the rain around the corner of the building to a big graveled parking lot.

The lights of a car blinked at him and his coupe slid along the wet gravel and pulled up. Tony Acosta was at the wheel.

Carmady got in at the right side and said: "Let's go out to Cyrano's and have a drink, Tony."

"Jeeze, that's swell. Miss Adrian's in the floor show there. You know, the blonde I told you about."

Carmady said: "I saw Targo. I kind of liked him—but I didn't like his clothes."

## 4

Gus Neishacker was a two-hundred-pound fashion plate with very red cheeks and thin, exquisitely penciled eyebrows—eyebrows from a Chinese vase. There was a red carnation in the lapel of his wide-shouldered dinner jacket and he kept sniffing at it while he watched the headwaiter seat a party of guests. When Carmady and Tony Acosta came through the foyer arch he flashed a sudden smile and went to them with his hand out.

"How's a boy, Ted? Party?"

Carmady said: "Just the two of us. Meet Mister Acosta. Gus Neishacker, Cyrano's floor manager."

Gus Neishacker shook hands with Tony without looking at him. He said: "Let's see, the last time you dropped in—"

"She left town," Carmady said. "We'll sit near the ring but not too near. We don't dance together."

Gus Neishacker jerked a menu from under the headwaiter's arm and led the way down five crimson steps, along the tables that skirted the oval dance floor.

They sat down. Carmady ordered rye highballs and Denver sandwiches. Neishacker gave the order to a waiter, pulled a chair out and sat down at the table. He took a pencil out and made triangles on the inside of a match cover.

"See the fights?" he asked carelessly.

"Was that what they were?"

Gus Neishacker smiled indulgently. "Benny talked to the Duke. He says you're wise." He looked suddenly at Tony Acosta.

"Tony's all right," Carmady said.

"Yeah. Well do us a favor, will you? See it stops right here. Benny likes this boy. He wouldn't let him get hurt. He'd put protection all around him—real protection—if he thought that threat stuff was anything but some pool-hall bum's idea of a very funny joke.

Benny never backs but one boxfighter at a time, and he picks them damn careful."

Carmady lit a cigarette, blew smoke from a corner of his mouth, said quietly: "It's none of my business, but I'm telling you it's screwy. I have a nose for that sort of thing."

Gus Neishacker stared at him a minute, then shrugged. He said: "I hope you're wrong," stood up quickly and walked away among the tables. He bent to smile here and there, and speak to a customer.

Tony Acosta's velvet eyes shone. He said: "Jeeze, Mister Carmady, you think it's rough stuff?"

Carmady nodded, didn't say anything. The waiter put their drinks and sandwiches on the table, went away. The band on the stage at the end of the oval floor blared out a long chord and a slick, grinning m.c. slid out on the stage and put his lips to a small open mike.

The floor show began. A line of half-naked girls ran out under a rain of colored lights. They coiled and uncoiled in a long sinuous line, their bare legs flashing, their navels little dimples of darkness in soft white, very nude flesh.

A hard-boiled redhead sang a hard-boiled song in a voice that could have been used to split firewood. The girls came back in black tights and silk hats, did the same dance with a slightly different exposure.

The music softened and a tall high-yaller torch singer drooped under an amber light and sang of something very far away and unhappy, in a voice like old ivory.

Carmady sipped his drink, poked at his sandwich in the dim light. Tony Acosta's hard young face was a small tense blur beside him.

The torch singer went away and there was a little pause and then suddenly all the lights in the place went out except the lights over the music racks of the band and little pale amber lights at the entrances to the radiating aisles of booths beyond the tables.

There were squeals in the thick darkness. A single

white spot winked on, high up under the roof, settled on a runway beside the stage. Faces were chalk-white in the reflected glare. There was the red glow of a cigarette tip here and there. Four tall black men moved in the light, carrying a white mummy case on their shoulders. They came slowly, in rhythm, down the runway. They wore white Egyptian headdresses and loincloths of white leather and white sandals laced to the knee. The black smoothness of their limbs was like black marble in the moonlight.

They reached the middle of the dance floor and slowly upended the mummy case until the cover tipped forward and fell and was caught. Then slowly, very slowly, a swathed white figure tipped forward and fell— slowly, like the last leaf from a dead tree. It tipped in the air, seemed to hover, then plunged towards the floor under a shattering roll of drums.

The light went off, went on. The swathed figure was upright on the floor, spinning, and one of the blacks was spinning the opposite way, winding the white shroud around his body. Then the shroud fell away and a girl was all tinsel and smooth white limbs under the hard light and her body shot through the air glittering and was caught and passed around swiftly among the four black men, like a baseball handled by a fast infield.

Then the music changed to a waltz and she danced among the black men slowly and gracefully, as though among four ebony pillars, very close to them but never touching them.

The act ended. The applause rose and fell in thick waves. The light went out and it was dark again, and then all the lights went up and the girl and the four black men were gone.

"Keeno," Tony Acosta breathed. "Oh, keeno. That was Miss Adrian, wasn't it?"

Carmady said slowly: "A little daring." He lit another

cigarette, looked around. "There's another black and white number, Tony. The Duke himself, in person."

Duke Targo stood applauding violently at the entrance to one of the radiating booth aisles. There was a loose grin on his face. He looked as if he might have had a few drinks.

An arm came down over Carmady's shoulder. A hand planted itself in the ash tray at his elbow. He smelled Scotch in heavy gusts. He turned his head slowly, looked up at the liquor-shiny face of Shenvair, Duke Targo's drunken bodyguard.

"Smokes and a white gal," Shenvair said thickly. "Lousy. Crummy. Godawful crummy."

Carmady smiled slowly, moved his chair a little. Tony Acosta stared at Shenvair round-eyed, his little mouth a thin line.

"Blackface, Mister Shenvair. Not real smokes. I liked it."

"And who the hell cares what you like?" Shenvair wanted to know.

Carmady smiled delicately, laid his cigarette down on the edge of a plate. He turned his chair a little more.

"Still think I want your job, Shenvair?"

"Yeah. I owe you a smack in the puss too." He took his hand out of the ash tray, wiped it off on the tablecloth. He doubled it into a fist. "Like it now?"

A waiter caught him by the arm, spun him around.

"You lost your table, sir? This way."

Shenvair patted the waiter on the shoulder, tried to put an arm around his neck. "Swell, let's go nibble a drink. I don't like these people."

They went away, disappeared among the tables.

Carmady said: "To hell with this place, Tony," and stared moodily towards the band stage. Then his eyes became intent.

A girl with corn-blond hair, in a white wrap with a white fur collar, appeared at the edge of the shell, went behind it, reappeared nearer. She came along the edge of the booths to the place where Targo had been standing. She slipped in between the booths there, disappeared.

Carmady said: "To hell with this place. Let's go Tony," in a low angry voice. Then very softly, in a tensed tone: "No—wait a minute. I see another guy I don't like."

The man was on the far side of the dance floor, which was empty at the moment. He was following its curve around, past the tables that fringed it. He looked a little different without his hat. But he had the same flat white expressionless face, the same close-set eyes. He was youngish, not more than thirty, but already having trouble with his bald spot. The slight bulge of a gun under his left arm was barely noticeable. He was the man who had run away from Jean Adrian's apartment in the Carondelet.

He reached the aisle into which Targo had gone, into which a moment before Jean Adrian had gone. He went into it.

Carmady said sharply: "Wait here, Tony." He kicked his chair back and stood up.

Somebody rabbit-punched him from behind. He swiveled, close to Shenvair's grinning sweaty face.

"Back again, pal," the curly-haired man chortled, and hit him on the jaw.

It was a short jab, well placed for a drunk. It caught Carmady off balance, staggered him. Tony Acosta came to his feet snarling, catlike. Carmady was still rocking when Shenvair let go with the other fist. That was too slow, too wide. Carmady slid inside it, uppercut the curly-haired man's nose savagely, got a handful of blood before he could get his hand away. He put most of it back on Shenvair's face.

Shenvair wobbled, staggered back a step and sat down on the floor, hard. He clapped a hand to his nose.

"Keep an eye on this bird, Tony," Carmady said swiftly.

Shenvair took hold of the nearest tablecloth and yanked it. It came off the table. Silver and glasses and china followed it to the floor. A man swore and a woman squealed. A waiter ran towards them with a livid, furious face.

Carmady almost didn't hear the two shots.

They were small and flat, close together, a small-caliber gun. The rushing waiter stopped dead, and a deeply etched white line appeared around his mouth as instantly as though the lash of a whip had cut it there.

A dark woman with a sharp nose opened her mouth to yell and no sound came from her. There was the instant when nobody makes a sound, when it almost seems as if there will never again be any sound—after the sound of a gun. Then Carmady was running.

He bumped into people who stood up and craned their necks. He reached the entrance to the aisle into which the white-faced man had gone. The booths had high walls and swing doors not so high. Heads stuck out over the doors, but no one was in the aisle yet. Carmady charged up a shallow carpeted slope, at the far end of which booth doors stood wide open.

Legs in dark cloth showed past the doors, slack on the floor, the knees sagged. The toes of black shoes were pointed into the booth.

Carmady shook an arm off, reached the place.

The man lay across the end of a table, his stomach and one side of his face on the white cloth, his left hand dropped between the table and the padded seat. His right hand on top of the table didn't quite hold a big black gun, a .45 with a cut barrel. The bald spot on his head glistened under the light, and the oily metal of the gun glistened beside it.

Blood leaked from under his chest, vivid scarlet on the white cloth, seeping into it as into blotting paper.

Duke Targo was standing up, deep in the booth. His left arm in the white serge coat was braced on the end of the table. Jean Adrian was sitting down at his side.

Targo looked at Carmady blankly, as if he had never seen him before. He pushed his big right hand forward.

A small white-handled automatic lay on his palm.

"I shot him," Targo said. He pulled a gun on us and I shot him."

Jean Adrian was scrubbing her hands together on a scrap of handkerchief. Her face was strained, cold, not scared. Her eyes were dark.

"I shot him," Targo said. He threw the small gun down on the cloth. It bounced, almost hit the fallen man's head. "Let's—let's get out of here."

Carmady put a hand against the side of the sprawled man's neck, held it there a second or two, took it away.

"He's dead," he said. "When a citizen drops a red-hot—that's news."

Jean Adrian was staring at him stiff-eyed. He flashed a smile at her, put a hand against Targo's chest, pushed him back.

"Sit down, Targo. You're not going any place."

Targo said: "Well—okey. I shot him, see."

"That's all right," Carmady said. "Just relax."

People were close behind him now, crowding him. He leaned back against the press of bodies and kept on smiling at the girl's white face.

## 5

Benny Cyrano was shaped like two eggs, a little one that was his head on top of a big one that was his body. His small dapper legs and feet in patent-leather shoes were pushed into the kneehole of a dark sheenless desk. He held a corner of a handkerchief tightly between his teeth and pulled against it with his left hand and held his right hand out pudgily in front of him, pushing against the air. He was saying in a voice muffled by the handkerchief: "Now wait a minute, boys. Now wait a minute."

There was a striped built-in sofa in one corner of the office, and Duke Targo sat in the middle of it, between two Headquarters dicks. He had a dark bruise over one cheekbone, his thick blond hair was tousled and his black satin shirt looked as if somebody had tried to swing him by it.

One of the dicks, the gray-haired one, had a split lip. The young one with hair as blond as Targo's had a black eye. They both looked mad, but the blond one looked madder.

Carmady straddled a chair against the wall and looked sleepily at Jean Adrian, near him in a leather rocker. She was twisting a handkerchief in her hands, rubbing her palms with it. She had been doing this for a long time, as if she had forgotten she was doing it. Her small firm mouth was angry.

Gus Neishacker leaned against the closed door smoking.

"Now wait a minute, boys," Cyrano said. "If you didn't get tough with him, he wouldn't fight back. He's a good boy—the best I ever had. Give him a break."

Blood dribbled from one corner of Targo's mouth, in a fine thread down to his jutting chin. It gathered there and glistened. His face was empty, expressionless.

Carmady said coldly: "You wouldn't want the boys to stop playing blackjack pinochle, would you, Benny?"

The blond dick snarled: "You still got that private-dick license, Carmady?"

"It's lying around somewhere, I guess," Carmady said.

"Maybe we could take it away from you," the blond dick snarled.

"Maybe you could do a fan dance, copper. You might be all kinds of a smart guy for all I'd know."

The blond dick started to get up. The older one said: "Leave him be. Give him six feet. If he steps over that, we'll take the screws out of him."

Carmady and Gus Neishacker grinned at each other.

Cyrano made helpless gestures in the air. The girl looked at Carmady under her lashes. Targo opened his mouth and spat blood straight before him on the blue carpet.

Something pushed against the door and Neishacker stepped to one side, opened it a crack, then opened it wide. McChesney came in.

McChesney was a lieutenant of detectives, tall, sandy-haired, fortyish, with pale eyes and a narrow suspicious face. He shut the door and turned the key in it, went slowly over and stood in front of Targo.

"Plenty dead," he said. "One under the heart, one in it. Nice snap shooting. In any league."

"When you've got to deliver you've got to deliver," Targo said dully.

"Make him?" the gray-haired dick asked his partner, moving away along the sofa.

McChesney nodded. "Torchy Plant. A gun for hire. I haven't seen him round for all of two years. Tough as an ingrowing toenail with his right load. A bindle punk."

"He'd have to be that to throw his party in here," the gray-haired dick said.

McChesney's long face was serious, not hard. "Got a permit for the gun, Targo?"

Targo said: "Yes. Benny got me one two weeks ago. I been getting a lot of threats."

"Listen, Lieutenant," Cyrano chirped, "some gamblers try to scare him into a dive, see? He wins nine straight fights by knockouts so they get a swell price. I told him he should take one at that maybe."

"I almost did," Targo said sullenly.

"So they sent the redhot to him," Cyrano said.

McChesney said: "I wouldn't say no. How'd you beat his draw, Targo? Where was your gun?"

"On my hip."

"Show me."

Targo put his hand back into his right hip pocket

and jerked a handkerchief out quickly, stuck his finger through it like a gun barrel.

"That handkerchief in the pocket?" McChesney asked. "With the gun?"

Targo's big reddish face clouded a little. He nodded.

McChesney leaned forward casually and twitched the handkerchief from his hand. He sniffed at it, unwrapped it, sniffed at it again, folded it and put it away in his own pocket. His face said nothing.

"What did he say, Targo?"

"He said: 'I got a message for you, punk, and this is it.' Then he went for the gat and it stuck a little in the clip. I got mine out first."

McChesney smiled faintly and leaned far back, teetering on his heels. His faint smile seemed to slide off the end of his long nose. He looked Targo up and down.

"Yeah," he said softly. "I'd call it damn nice shooting with a twenty-two. But you're fast for a big guy . . . Who got these threats?"

"I did," Targo said. "Over the phone."

"Know the voice?"

"It might have been this same guy. I'm not just positive."

McChesney walked stiff-legged to the other end of the office, stood a moment looking at a hand-tinted sporting print. He came back slowly, drifted over to the door.

"A guy like that don't mean a lot," he said quietly, "but we got to do our job. The two of you will have to come downtown and make statements. Let's go."

He went out. The two dicks stood up, with Duke Targo between them. The gray-haired one snapped: "You goin' to act nice, bo?"

Targo sneered: "If I get to wash my face."

They went out. The blond dick waited for Jean Adrian to pass in front of him. He swung the door, snarled back at Carmady: "As for you—nuts!"

Carmady said softly: "I like them. It's the squirrel in me, copper."

Gus Neishacker laughed, then shut the door and went to the desk.

"I'm shaking like Benny's third chin," he said. "Let's all have a shot of cognac."

He poured three glasses a third full, took one over to the striped sofa and spread his long legs out on it, leaned his head back and sipped the brandy.

Carmady stood up and downed his drink. He got a cigarette out and rolled it around in his fingers, staring at Cyrano's smooth white face with an up-from-under look.

"How much would you say changed hands on that fight tonight?" he asked softly. "Bets."

Cyrano blinked, massaged his lips with a fat hand. "A few grand. It was just a regular weekly show. It don't listen, does it?"

Carmady put the cigarette in his mouth and leaned over the desk to strike a match. He said: "If it does, murder's getting awfully cheap in this town."

Cyrano didn't say anything. Gus Neishacker sipped the last of his brandy and carefully put the empty glass down on a round cork table beside the sofa. He stared at the ceiling, silently.

After a moment Carmady nodded at the two men, crossed the room and went out, closed the door behind him. He went along a corridor off which dressing rooms opened, dark now. A curtained archway let him out at the back of the stage.

In the foyer the headwaiter was standing at the glass doors, looking out at the rain and the back of a uniformed policeman. Carmady went into the empty cloakroom, found his hat and coat, put them on, came out to stand beside the headwaiter.

He said: "I guess you didn't notice what happened to the kid I was with?"

The headwaiter shook his head and reached forward to unlock the door.

"There was four hundred people here—and three hundred scrammed before the law checked in. I'm sorry."

Carmady nodded and went out into the rain. The uniformed man glanced at him casually. He went along the street to where the car had been left. It wasn't there. He looked up and down the street, stood for a few moments in the rain, then walked towards Melrose.

After a little while he found a taxi.

## 6

The ramp of the Carondelet garage curved down into semi-darkness and chilled air. The dark bulks of stalled cars looked ominous against the whitewashed walls, and the single droplight in the small office had the relentless glitter of the death house.

A big Negro in stained overalls came out rubbing his eyes, then his face split in an enormous grin.

"Hello, there, Mistuh Carmady. You kinda restless tonight?"

Carmady said: "I get a little wild when it rains. I bet my heap isn't here."

"No, it ain't, Mistuh Carmady. I been all around wipin' off and yours ain't here aytall."

Carmady said woodenly: "I lent it to a pal. He probably wrecked it . . ."

He flicked a half-dollar through the air and went back up the ramp to the side street. He turned towards the back of the hotel, came to an alleylike street one side of which was the rear wall of the Carondelet. The other side had two frame houses and a four-story brick building. Hotel Blaine was lettered on a round milky globe over the door.

Carmady went up three cement steps and tried the

door. It was locked. He looked through the glass panel into a small dim empty lobby. He got out two passkeys; the second one moved the lock a little. He pulled the door hard towards him, tried the first one again. That snicked the bolt far enough for the loosely fitted door to open.

He went in and looked at an empty counter with a sign "Manager" beside a plunger bell. There was an oblong of empty numbered pigeonholes on the wall. Carmady went around behind the counter and fished a leather register out of a space under the top. He read names back three pages, found the boyish scrawl: "Tony Acosta," and a room number in another writing.

He put the register away and went past the automatic elevator and upstairs to the fourth floor.

The hallway was very silent. There was weak light from a ceiling fixture. The last door but one on the left-hand side had a crack of light showing around its transom. That was the door—411. He put his hand out to knock, then withdrew it without touching the door.

The doorknob was heavily smeared with something that looked like blood.

Carmady's eyes looked down and saw what was almost a pool of blood on the stained wood before the door, beyond the edge of the runner.

His hand suddenly felt clammy inside his glove. He took the glove off, held the hand stiff, clawlike for a moment, then shook it slowly. His eyes had a sharp strained light in them.

He got a handkerchief out, grasped the doorknob inside it, turned it slowly. The door was unlocked. He went in.

He looked across the room and said very softly: "Tony . . . oh, Tony."

Then he shut the door behind him and turned a key in it, still with the handkerchief.

There was light from the bowl that hung on three brass chains from the middle of the ceiling. It shone on a made-up bed, some painted, light-colored furniture, a dull green carpet, a square writing desk of eucalyptus wood.

Tony Acosta sat at the desk. His head was slumped forward on his left arm. Under the chair on which he sat, between the legs of the chair and his feet, there was a glistening brownish pool.

Carmady walked across the room so rigidly that his ankles ached after the second step. He reached the desk, touched Tony Acosta's shoulder.

"Tony," he said thickly, in a low, meaningless voice. "My God, Tony!"

Tony didn't move. Carmady went around to his side. A blood-soaked bath towel glared against the boy's stomach, across his pressed-together thighs. His right hand was crouched against the front edge of the desk, as if he was trying to push himself up. Almost under his face there was a scrawled envelope.

Carmady pulled the envelope towards him slowly, lifted it like a thing of weight, read the wandering scrawl of words.

"Tailed him . . . woptown . . . 28 Court Street . . . over garage . . . shot me . . . think I got . . . him . . . your car . . ."

The line trailed over the edge of the paper, became a blot there. The pen was on the floor. There was a bloody thumbprint on the envelope.

Carmady folded it meticulously to protect the print, put the envelope in his wallet. He lifted Tony's head, turned it a little towards him. The neck was still warm; it was beginning to stiffen. Tony's soft dark eyes were open and they held the quiet brightness of a cat's eyes. They had that effect the eyes of the new-dead have of almost, but not quite, looking at you.

Carmady lowered the head gently on the outstretched left arm. He stood laxly, his head on one side, his eyes almost sleepy. Then his head jerked back and his eyes hardened.

He stripped off his raincoat and the suitcoat underneath, rolled his sleeves up, wet a face towel in the basin in the corner of the room and went to the door. He wiped the knobs off, bent down and wiped up the smeared blood from the floor outside.

He rinsed the towel and hung it up to dry, wiped his hands carefully, put his coat on again. He used his handkerchief to open the transom, to reverse the key and lock the door from the outside. He threw the key in over the top of the transom, heard it tinkle inside.

He went downstairs and out of the Hotel Blaine. It still rained. He walked to the corner, looked along a tree-shaded block. His car was a dozen yards from the intersection, parked carefully, the lights off, the keys in the ignition. He drew them out, felt the seat under the wheel. It was wet, sticky. Carmady wiped his hand off, ran the windows up and locked the car. He left it where it was.

Going back to the Carondelet he didn't meet anybody. The hard slanting rain still pounded down into the empty streets.

7

There was a thin thread of light under the door of 914. Carmady knocked lightly, looking up and down the hall, moved his gloved fingers softly on the panel while he waited. He waited a long time. Then a voice spoke wearily behind the wood of the door.

"Yes?" What is it?"

"Carmady, angel. I have to see you. It's strictly business."

The door clicked, opened. He looked at a tired white face, dark eyes that were slatelike, not violet-blue. There were smudges under them as though mascara had been rubbed into the skin. The girl's strong little hand twitched on the edge of the door.

"You," she said wearily. "It would be you. Yes . . . Well, I've simply got to have a shower. I smell of policemen."

"Fifteen minutes?" Carmady asked casually, but his eyes were very sharp on her face.

She shrugged slowly, then nodded. The closing door seemed to jump at him. He went along to his own rooms, threw off his hat and coat, poured whiskey into a glass and went into the bathroom to get ice water from the small tap over the basin.

He drank slowly, looking out of the windows at the dark breadth of the boulevard. A car slid by now and then, two beams of white light attached to nothing, emanating from nowhere.

He finished the drink, stripped to the skin, went under a shower. He dressed in fresh clothes, refilled his big flask and put it in his inner pocket, took a snub-nosed automatic out of a suitcase and held it in his hand for a minute staring at it. Then he put it back in the suitcase, lit a cigarette and smoked it through.

He got a dry hat and a tweed coat and went back to 914.

The door was almost insidiously ajar. He slipped in with a light knock, shut the door, went on into the living room and looked at Jean Adrian.

She was sitting on the davenport with a freshly scrubbed look, in loose plum-colored pajamas and a Chinese coat. A tendril of damp hair drooped over one temple. Her small even features had the cameo-like clearness that tiredness gives to the very young.

Carmady said: "Drink?"

She gestured emptily. "I suppose so."

He got glasses, mixed whiskey and ice water, went to the davenport with them.

"Are they keeping Targo on ice?"

She moved her chin an eighth of an inch, staring into her glass.

"He cut loose again, knocked two cops halfway through the wall. They love that boy."

Carmady said: "He has a lot to learn about cops. In the morning the cameras will be all set for him. I can think of some nice headlines, such as: "Well-known Fighter Too Fast for Gunman." "Duke Targo Puts Crimp in Underworld Hot Rod.""

The girl sipped her drink. "I'm tired," she said. "And my foot itches. Let's talk about what makes this your business."

"Sure." He flipped his cigarette case open, held it under her chin. Her hand fumbled at it and while it still fumbled he said: "When you light that tell me why you shot him."

Jean Adrian put the cigarette between her lips, bent her head to the match, inhaled and threw her head back. Color awakened slowly in her eyes and a small smile curved the line of her pressed lips. She didn't answer.

Carmady watched her for a minute, turning his glass in his hands. Then he stared at the floor, said: "It was your gun—the gun I picked up here in the afternoon. Targo said he drew it from his hip pocket, the slowest draw in the world. Yet he's supposed to have shot twice, accurately enough to kill a man, while the man wasn't even getting his gun loose from a shoulder holster. That's hooey. But you, with the gun in a bag in your lap, and knowing the hood, might just have managed it. He would have been watching Targo."

The girl said emptily: "You're a private dick, I hear. You're the son of a boss politician. They talked about you downtown. They act a little afraid of you, of people who might know. Who sicked you on me?"

Carmady said: "They're not afraid of me, angel. They just talked like that to see how you'd react, if I was involved, so on. They don't know what it's all about."

"They were told plainly enough what it was all about."

Carmady shook his head. "A cop never believes what he gets without a struggle. He's too used to cooked-up stories. I think McChesney's wise you did the shooting. He knows by now if that handkerchief of Targo's had been in a pocket with a gun."

Her limp fingers discarded her cigarette half-smoked. A curtain eddied at the window and loose flakes of ash crawled around in the ash tray. She said slowly: "All right. I shot him. Do you think I'd hesitate after this afternoon?"

Carmady rubbed the lobe of his ear. "I'm playing this too light," he said softly. "You don't know what's in my heart. Something has happened, something nasty. Do you think the hood meant to kill Targo?"

"I thought so—or I wouldn't have shot a man."

"I think maybe it was just a scare, angel. Like the other one. After all a night club is a poor place for a getaway."

She said sharply: "They don't do many low tackles on forty-fives. He'd have got away all right. Of course he meant to kill somebody. And of course I didn't mean Duke to front for me. He just grabbed the gun out of my hand and slammed into his act. What did it matter? I knew it would all come out in the end."

She poked absently at the still burning cigarette in the tray, kept her eyes down. After a moment she said, almost in a whisper: "Is that all you wanted to know?"

Carmady let his eyes crawl sidewise, without moving his head, until he could just see the firm curve of her cheek, the strong line of her throat. He said thickly: "Shenvair was in on it. The fellow I was with at Cyrano's followed Shenvair to a hideout. Shenvair shot him. He's dead. He's dead, angel—just a young kid that worked here in the hotel. Tony, the bell captain. The cops don't know that yet."

The muffled clang of elevator doors was heavy through the silence. A horn tooted dismally out in the rain on the boulevard. The girl sagged forward sudden-

ly, then sidewise, fell across Carmady's knees. Her
body was half turned and she lay almost on her back
across his thighs, her eyelids flickering. The small blue
veins in them stood out rigid in the soft skin.

He put his arms around her slowly, loosely, then
they tightened, lifted her. He brought her face close to
his own face. He kissed her on the side of the mouth.

Her eyes opened, stared blankly, unfocused. He
kissed her again, tightly, then pushed her upright on the
davenport.

He said quietly: "That wasn't just an act, was it?"

She leaped to her feet, spun around. Her voice was
low, tense and angry.

"There's something horrible about you! Something—
satanic. You come here and tell me another man has
been killed—and then you kiss me. It isn't real."

Carmady said dully: "There's something horrible
about any man that goes suddenly gaga over another
man's woman."

"I'm not his woman!" she snapped. "I don't even
like him—and I don't like you."

Carmady shrugged. They stared at each other with
bleak hostile eyes. The girl clicked her teeth shut, then
said almost violently: "Get out! I can't talk to you any
more. I can't stand you around. Will you get out?"

Carmady said: "Why not?" He stood up, went over
and got his hat and coat.

The girl sobbed once sharply, then she went in light
quick strides across the room to the windows, became
motionless with her back to him.

Carmady looked at her back, went over near her and
stood looking at the soft hair low down on her neck. He
said: "Why the hell don't you let me help? I know
there's something wrong. I wouldn't hurt you."

The girl spoke to the curtain in front of her face,
savagely: "Get out! I don't want your help. Go away
and stay away. I won't be seeing you—ever."

Carmady said slowly: "I think you've got to have

help. Whether you like it or not. That man in the photo frame on the desk there—I think I know who he is. And I don't think he's dead."

The girl turned. Her face now was as white as paper. Her eyes strained at his eyes. She breathed thickly, harshly. After what seemed a long time she said: "I'm caught. Caught. There's nothing you can do about it."

Carmady lifted a hand and drew his fingers slowly down her cheek, down the angle of her tight jaw. His eyes held a hard brown glitter, his lips a smile. It was cunning, almost a dishonest smile.

He said: "I'm wrong, angel. I don't know him at all. Good night."

He went back across the room, through the little hallway, opened the door. When the door opened the girl clutched at the curtain and rubbed her face against it slowly.

Carmady didn't shut the door. He stood quite still halfway through it, looking at two men who stood there with guns.

They stood close to the door, as if they had been about to knock. One was thick, dark, saturnine. The other one was an albino with sharp red eyes, a narrow head that showed shining snow-white hair under a rain-spattered dark hat. He had the thin sharp teeth and the drawn-back grin of a rat.

Carmady started to close the door behind him. The albino said: "Hold it, rube. The door, I mean. We're goin' in."

The other man slid forward and pressed his left hand up and down Carmady's body carefully. He stepped away, said: "No gat, but a swell flask under his arm."

The albino gestured with his gun. "Back up, rube. We want the broad, too."

Carmady said tonelessly: "It doesn't take a gun, Critz. I know you and I know your boss. If he wants to see me, I'll be glad to talk to him."

He turned and went back into the room with the two gunmen behind him.

Jean Adrian hadn't moved. She stood by the window still, the curtain against her cheek, her eyes closed, as if she hadn't heard the voices at the door at all.

Then she heard them come in and her eyes snapped open. She turned slowly, stared past Carmady at the two gunmen. The albino walked to the middle of the room, looked around it without speaking, went on into the bedroom and bathroom. Doors opened and shut. He came back in quiet catlike feet, pulled his overcoat open and pushed his hat back on his head.

"Get dressed, sister. We have to go for a ride in the rain. Okey?"

The girl stared at Carmady now. He shrugged, smiled a little, spread his hands.

"That's how it is, angel. Might as well fall in line."

The lines of her face got thin and contemptuous. She said slowly: "You—You——." Her voice trailed off into a sibilant, meaningless mutter. She went across the room stiffly and out of it into the bedroom.

The albino slipped a cigarette between his sharp lips, chuckled with a wet, gurgling sound, as if his mouth was full of saliva.

"She don't seem to like you, rube."

Carmady frowned. He walked slowly to the writing desk, leaned his hips against it, stared at the floor.

"She thinks I sold her out," he said dully.

"Maybe you did, rube," the albino drawled.

Carmady said: "Better watch her. She's neat with a gun."

His hands, reaching casually behind him on the desk, tapped the top of it lightly, then without apparent change of movement folded the leather photo frame down on its side and edged it under the blotter.

## 8

There was a padded arm rest in the middle of the rear seat of the car, and Carmady leaned an elbow on it, cupped his chin in his hand, stared through the half-misted windows at the rain. It was thick white spray in the headlights, and the noise of it on the top of the car was like drum fire very far off.

Jean Adrian sat on the other side of the arm rest, in the corner. She wore a black hat and a gray coat with tufts of silky hair on it, longer than caracul and not so curly. She didn't look at Carmady or speak to him.

The albino sat on the right of the thick dark man, who drove. They went through silent streets, past blurred houses, blurred trees, the blurred shine of street lights. There were neon signs behind the thick curtains of mist. There was no sky.

Then they climbed and a feeble arc light strung over an intersection threw light on a signpost, and Carmady read the name "Court Street."

He said softly: "This is woptown, Critz. The big guy can't be so dough-heavy as he used to be."

Lights flickered from the albino's eyes as he glanced back. "You should know, rube."

The car slowed in front of a big frame house with a trellised porch, walls finished in round shingles, blind, lightless windows. Across the street, a stencil sign on a brick building built sheer to the sidewalk said: "Paolo Perrugini Funeral Parlors."

The car swung out to make a wide turn into a gravel driveway. Lights splashed into an open garage. They went in, slid to a stop beside a big shiny undertaker's ambulance.

The albino snapped: "All out!"

Carmady said: "I see our next trip is all arranged for."

"Funny guy," the albino snarled. "A wise monkey."

"Uh-uh. I just have nice scaffold manners," Carmady drawled.

The dark man cut the motor and snapped on a big flash, then cut the lights, got out of the car. He shot the beam of the flash up a narrow flight of wooden steps in the corner. The albino said: "Up you go, rube. Push the girl ahead of you. I'm behind with my rod."

Jean Adrian got out of the car past Carmady, without looking at him. She went up the steps stiffly, and the three men made a procession behind her.

There was a door at the top. The girl opened it and hard white light came out at them. They went into a bare attic with exposed studding, a square window in front and rear, shut tight, the glass painted black. A bright bulb hung on a drop cord over a kitchen table and a big man sat at the table with a saucer of cigarette butts at his elbow. Two of them still smoked.

A thin loose-lipped man sat on a bed with a Luger beside his left hand. There was a worn carpet on the floor, a few sticks of furniture, a half-opened clapboard door in the corner through which a toilet seat showed, and one end of a big old-fashioned bathtub standing up from the floor on iron legs.

The man at the kitchen table was large but not handsome. He had carroty hair and eyebrows a shade darker, a square aggressive face, a strong jaw. His thick lips held his cigarette brutally. His clothes looked as if they had cost a great deal of money and had been slept in.

He glanced carelessly at Jean Adrian, said around the cigarette: "Park the body, sister. Hi, Carmady. Gimme that rod, Lefty, and you boys drop down below again."

The girl went quietly across the attic and sat down in a straight wooden chair. The man on the bed stood up, put the Luger at the big man's elbow on the kitchen table. The three gunmen went down the stairs, leaving the door open.

The big man touched the Luger, stared at Carmady, said sarcastically: "I'm Doll Conant. Maybe you remember me."

Carmady stood loosely by the kitchen table, with his legs spread wide, his hands in his overcoat pockets, his head tilted back. His half-closed eyes were sleepy, very cold.

He said: "Yeah. I helped my dad hang the only rap on you that ever stuck."

"It didn't stick, mugg. Not with the Court of Appeals."

"Maybe this one will," Carmady said carelessly. "Kidnapping is apt to be a sticky rap in this state."

Conant grinned without opening his lips. His expression was grimly good-humored. He said: "Let's not barber. We got business to do and you know better than that last crack. Sit down—or rather take a look at Exhibit One first. In the bathtub, behind you. Yeah, take a look at that. Then we can get down to tacks."

Carmady turned, went across to the clapboard door, pushed through it. There was a bulb sticking out of the wall, with a key switch. He snapped it on, bent over the tub.

For a moment his body was quite rigid and his breath was held rigidly. Then he let it out very slowly, and reached his left hand back and pushed the door almost shut. He bent farther over the big iron tub.

It was long enough for a man to stretch out in, and a man was stretched out in it, on his back. He was fully dressed even to a hat, although his had didn't look as if he had put it on himself. He had thick, gray-brown curly hair. There was blood on his face and there was a gouged, red-rimmed hole at the inner corner of his left eye.

He was Shenvair and he was long since dead.

Carmady sucked in his breath and straightened slowly, then suddenly bent forward still further until he could see into the space between the tub and the wall.

Something blue and metallic glistened down there in the dust. A blue steel gun. A gun like Shenvair's gun.

Carmady glanced back quickly. The not quite shut door showed him a part of the attic, the top of the stairs, one of Doll Conant's feet square and placid on the carpet, under the kitchen table. He reached his arm out slowly down behind the tub, gathered the gun up. The four exposed chambers had steel-jacketed bullets in them.

Carmady opened his coat, slipped the gun down inside the waistband of his trousers, tightened his belt, and buttoned his coat again. He went out of the bathroom, shut the clapboard door carefully.

Doll Conant gestured at a chair across the table from him: "Sit down."

Carmady glanced at Jean Adrian. She was staring at him with a kind of rigid curiosity, her eyes dark and colorless in a stone-white face under the black hat.

He gestured at her, smiled faintly. "It's Mister Shenvair, angel. He met with an accident. He's—dead."

The girl stared at him without any expression at all. Then she shuddered once, violently. She stared at him again, made no sound of any kind.

Carmady sat down in the chair across the table from Conant.

Conant eyed him, added a smoking stub to the collection in the white saucer, lit a fresh cigarette, streaking the match the whole length of the kitchen table.

He puffed, said casually: "Yeah, he's dead. You shot him."

Carmady shook his head very slightly, smiled. "No."

"Skip the baby eyes, feller. You shot him. Perrugini, the wop undertaker across the street, owns this place, rents it out now and then to a right boy for a quick dust. Incidentally, he's a friend of mine, does me a lot of good among the other wops. He rented it to Shenvair. Didn't know him, but Shenvair got a right ticket into him. Perrugini heard shooting over here tonight, took a look out of his window, saw a guy make it to a car. He saw the license number of the car. Your car."

Carmady shook his head again. "But I didn't shoot him, Conant."

"Try and prove it . . . The wop ran over and found Shenvair halfway up the stairs, dead. He dragged him up and stuck him in the bathtub. Some crazy idea about the blood, I suppose. Then he went through him, found a police card, a private-dick license, and that scared him. He got me on the phone and when I got the name, I came steaming."

Conant stopped talking, eyed Carmady steadily. Carmady said very softly: "You hear about the shooting at Cyrano's tonight?"

Conant nodded.

Carmady went on: "I was there, with a kid friend of mine from the hotel. Just before the shooting this Shenvair threw a punch at me. The kid followed Shenvair here and they shot each other. Shenvair was drunk and scared and I'll bet he shot first. I didn't even know the kid had a gun. Shenvair shot him through the stomach. He got home, died there. He left me a note. I have the note."

After a moment Conant said: "You killed Shenvair, or hired that boy to do it. Here's why. He tried to copper his bet on your blackmail racket. He sold out to Courtway."

Carmady looked startled. He snapped his head around to look at Jean Adrian. She was leaning forward staring at him with color in her cheeks, a shine in her eyes. She said very softly: "I'm sorry—angel. I had you wrong."

Carmady smiled a little, turned back to Conant. He said: "She thought I was the one that sold out. Who's Courtway? Your bird dog, the state senator?"

Conant's face turned a little white. He laid his cigarette down very carefully in the saucer, leaned across the table and hit Carmady in the mouth with his fist.

Carmady went over backwards in the rickety chair. His head struck the floor.

Jean Adrian stood up quietly and her teeth made a sharp clicking sound. Then she didn't move.

Carmady rolled over on his side and got up and set the chair upright. He got a handkerchief out, patted his mouth, looked at the handkerchief.

Steps clattered on the stairs and the albino poked his narrow head into the room, poked a gun still farther in.

"Need any help, boss?"

Without looking at him, Conant said: "Get out—and shut that door—and stay out!"

The door was shut. The albino's steps died down the stairs. Carmady put his left hand on the back of the chair and moved it slowly back and forth. His right hand still held the handkerchief. His lips were getting puffed and darkish. His eyes looked at the Luger by Conant's elbow.

Conant picked up his cigarette and put it in his mouth. He said: "Maybe you think I'm going to neck this blackmail racket. I'm not, brother. I'm going to kill it—so it'll stay killed. You're going to spill your guts. I have three boys downstairs who need exercise. Get busy and talk."

Carmady said: "Yeah—but your three boys are downstairs." He slipped the handkerchief inside his coat. His hand came out with the blued gun in it. He said: "Take that Luger by the barrel and push it across the table so I can reach it."

Conant didn't move. His eyes narrowed to slits. His hard mouth jerked the cigarette in it once. He didn't touch the Luger. After a moment he said: "Guess you know what will happen to you now."

Carmady shook his head slightly. He said: "Maybe I'm not particular about that. If it does happen, you won't know anything about it."

Conant stared at him, didn't move. He stared at him

for quite a long time, stared at the blue gun. "Where did you get it? Didn't the heels frisk you?"

Carmady said: "They did. This is Shenvair's gun. Your wop friend must have kicked it behind the bathtub. Careless."

Conant reached two thick fingers forward and turned the Luger around and pushed it to the far edge of the table. He nodded and said tonelessly: "I lose this hand. I ought to have thought of that. That makes me do the talking."

Jean Adrian came quickly across the room and stood at the end of the table. Carmady reached forward across the chair and took the Luger in his left hand and slipped it down into his overcoat pocket, kept his hand on it. He rested the hand holding the blue gun on the top of the chair.

Jean Adrian said: "Who is this man?"

"Doll Conant, a local bigtimer. Senator John Myerson Courtway is his pipe line into the state senate. And Senator Courtway, angel, it the man in your photo frame on your desk. The man you said was your father, that you said was dead."

The girl said very quietly: "He is my father. I knew he wasn't dead. I'm blackmailing him—for a hundred grand. Shenvair and Targo and I. He never married my mother, so I'm illegitimate. But I'm still his child. I have rights and he won't recognize them. He treated my mother abominably, left her without a nickel. He had detectives watch me for years. Shenvair was one of them. He recognized my photos when I came here and met Targo. He remembered. He went up to San Francisco and got a copy of my birth certificate. I have it here."

She fumbled at her bag, felt around in it, opened a small zipper pocket in the lining. Her hand came out with a folded paper. She tossed it on the table.

Conant stared at her, reached a hand for the paper,

spread it out and studied it. He said slowly: "This doesn't prove anything."

Carmady took his left hand out of his pocket and reached for the paper. Conant pushed it towards him.

It was a certified copy of a birth certificate, dated originally in 1912. It recorded the birth of a girl child, Adriana Gianni Myerson, to John and Antonina Gianni Myerson. Carmady dropped the paper again.

He said: "Adriana Gianni—Jean Adrian. Was that the tip-off, Conant?"

Conant shook his head. "Shenvair got cold feet. He tipped Courtway. He was scared. That's why he had this hideout lined up. I thought that was why he got killed. Targo couldn't have done it, because Targo's still in the can. Maybe I had you wrong, Carmady."

Carmady stared at him woodenly, didn't say anything. Jean Adrian said: "It's my fault. I'm the one that's to blame. It was pretty rotten. I see that now. I want to see him and tell him I'm sorry and that he'll never hear from me again. I want to make him promise he won't do anything to Duke Targo. May I?"

Carmady said: "You can do anything you want to, angel. I have two guns that say so. But why did you wait so long? And why didn't you go at him through the courts? You're in show business. The publicity would have made you—even if he beat you out."

The girl bit her lip, said in a low voice: "My mother never really knew who he was, never knew his last name even. He was John Myerson to her. I didn't know until I came here and happened to see a picture in the local paper. He had changed, but I knew the face. And of course the first part of his name—"

Conant said sneeringly: "You didn't go at him openly because you knew damn well you weren't his kid. That your mother just wished you on to him like any cheap broad who sees herself out of a swell meal ticket. Courtway says he can prove it, and that he's going to prove it and put you where you belong. And believe me, sister, he's just the stiff-necked kind of sap who would kill himself in public life raking up a twenty-year-old scandal to do that little thing."

The big man spit his cigarette stub out viciously, added: "It cost me money to put him where he is and I aim to keep him there. That's why I'm in it. No dice, sister. I'm putting the pressure on. You're going to take a lot of air and keep on taking it. As for your two-gun friend—maybe he didn't know, but he knows now and that ties him up in the same package."

Conant banged on the table top, leaned back, looking calmly at the blue gun in Carmady's hand.

Carmady stared into the big man's eyes, said very softly: "That hood at Cyrano's tonight—he wasn't your idea of putting on the pressure by any chance, Conant, was he?"

Conant grinned harshly, shook his head. The door at the top of the stairs opened a little, silently. Carmady didn't see it. He was staring at Conant. Jean Adrian saw it.

Her eyes widened and she stepped back with a startled exclamation, that jerked Carmady's eyes to her.

The albino stepped softly through the door with a gun leveled.

His red eyes glistened, his mouth was drawn wide in a snarling grin. He said: "The door's kind of thin, boss. I listened. Okey? . . . Shed the heater, rube, or I blow you both in half."

Carmady turned slightly and opened his right hand and let the blue gun bounce on the thin carpet. He shrugged, spread his hands out wide, didn't look at Jean Adrian.

The albino stepped clear of the door, came slowly forward and put his gun against Carmady's back.

Conant stood up, came around the table, took the Luger out of Carmady's coat pocket and hefted it. Without a word or change of expression he slammed it against the side of Carmady's jaw.

Carmady sagged drunkenly, then went down on the floor on his side.

Jean Adrian screamed, clawed at Conant. He threw her off, changed the gun to his left hand and slapped the side of her face with a hard palm.

"Pipe down, sister. You've had all your fun."

The albino went to the head of the stairs and called down it. The two other gunmen came up into the room, stood grinning.

Carmady didn't move on the floor. After a little while Conant lit another cigarette and rattled a knuckle on the table top beside the birth certificate. He said gruffly: "She wants to see the old man. Okey, she can see him. We'll all go see him. There's still something in this that stinks." He raised his eyes, looked at the stocky man. "You and Lefty go downtown and spring Targo, get him out to the Senator's place as soon as you can. Step on it."

The two hoods went back down the stairs.

Conant looked down at Carmady, kicked him in the ribs lightly, kept on kicking them until Carmady opened his eyes and stirred.

## 9

The car waited at the top of a hill, before a pair of tall wrought-iron gates, inside which there was a lodge. A door of the lodge stood open and yellow light framed a big man in an overcoat and pulled-down hat. He came forward slowly into the rain, his hands down in his pockets.

The rain slithered about his feet and the albino leaned against the uprights of the gate, clicking his teeth. The big man said: "What yuh want? I can see yuh."

"Shake it up, rube. Mister Conant wants to call on your boss."

The man inside spat into the wet darkness. "So what? Know what time it is?"

Conant opened the car door suddenly and went over to the gates. The rain made noise between the car and the voices.

Carmady turned his head slowly and patted Jean Adrian's hand. She pushed his hand away from her quickly.

Her voice said softly: "You fool—oh, you fool!"

Carmady sighed. "I'm having a swell time, angel. A swell time."

The man inside the gates took out keys on a long chain, unlocked the gates and pushed them back until they clicked on the chocks. Conant and the albino came back to the car.

Conant stood in the rain with a heel hooked on the running board. Carmady took his big flask out of his pocket, felt it over to see if it was dented, then unscrewed the top. He held it out towards the girl, said: "Have a little bottle courage."

She didn't answer him, didn't move. He drank from the flask, put it away, looked past Conant's broad back at acres of dripping trees, a cluster of lighted windows that seemed to hang in the sky.

A car came up the hill stabbing the wet dark with its headlights, pulled behind the sedan and stopped. Conant went over to it, put his head into it and said something. The car backed, turned into the driveway, and its lights splashed on retaining walls, disappeared, reappeared at the top of the drive as a hard white oval against a stone porte-cochère.

Conant got into the sedan and the albino swung it into the driveway after the other car. At the top, in a cement parking circle ringed with cypresses, they all got out.

At the top of steps a big door was open and a man in a bathrobe stood in it. Targo, between two men who leaned hard against him, was halfway up the steps. He

was bareheaded and without an overcoat. His big body
in the white coat looked enormous between the two
gunmen.

The rest of the party went up the steps and into the
house and followed the bathrobed butler down a hall
lined with portraits of somebody's ancestors, through a
still oval foyer to another hall and into a paneled study
with soft lights and heavy drapes and deep leather
chairs.

A man stood behind a big dark desk that was set in
an alcove made by low, outjutting bookcases. He was
enormously tall and thin. His white hair was so thick
and fine that no single hair was visible in it. He had a
small straight bitter mouth, black eyes without depth in
a white lined face. He stooped a little and a blue cordu-
roy bathrobe faced with satin was wrapped around his
almost freakish thinness.

The butler shut the door and Conant opened it again
and jerked his chin at the two men who had come in
with Targo. They went out. The albino stepped behind
Targo and pushed him down into a chair. Targo looked
dazed, stupid. There was a smear of dirt on one side of
his face and his eyes had a drugged look.

The girl went over to him quickly, said: "Oh, Duke—
are you all right, Duke?"

Targo blinked at her, half-grinned. "So you had to
rat, huh? Skip it. I'm fine." His voice had an unnatural
sound.

Jean Adrian went away from him and sat down and
hunched herself together as if she was cold.

The tall man stared coldly at everyone in the room in
turn, then said lifelessly: "Are these the blackmailers—
and was it necessary to bring them here in the middle
of the night?"

Conant shook himself out of his coat, threw it on the
floor behind a lamp. He lit a fresh cigarette and stood
spread-legged in the middle of the room, a big, rough,
rugged man very sure of himself. He said: "The girl

wanted to see you and tell you she was sorry and wants to play ball. The guy in the ice-cream coat is Targo, the fighter. He got himself in a shooting scrape at a night spot and acted so wild downtown they fed him sleep tablets to quiet him. The other guy is Carmady, old Marcus Carmady's boy. I don't figure him yet."

Carmady said dryly: "I'm a private detective, Senator. I'm here in the interests of my client, Miss Adrian." He laughed.

The girl looked at him suddenly, then looked at the floor.

Conant said gruffly. "Shenvair, the one you know about, got himself bumped off. Not by us. That's still to straighten out."

The tall man nodded coldly. He sat down at his desk and picked up a white quill pen, tickled one ear with it.

"And what is your idea of the way to handle this matter, Conant?" he asked thinly.

Conant shrugged. "I'm a rough boy, but I'd handle this one legal. Talk to the D.A., toss them in a coop on suspicion of extortion. Cook up a story for the papers, then give it time to cool. Then dump these birds across the state line and tell them not to come back—or else."

Senator Courtway moved the quill around to his other ear. "They could attack me again, from a distance," he said icily. "I'm in favor of a showdown, put them where they belong."

"You can't try them, Courtway. It would kill you politically."

"I'm tired of public life, Conant. I'll be glad to retire." The tall thin man curved his mouth into a faint smile.

"The hell you are," Conant growled. He jerked his head around, snapped: "Come here, sister."

Jean Adrian stood up, came slowly across the room, stood in front of the desk.

"Make her?" Conant snarled.

Courtway stared at the girl's set face for a long time,

without a trace of expression. He put his quill down on the desk, opened a drawer and took out a photograph. He looked from the photo to the girl, back to the photo, said tonelessly: "This was taken a number of years ago, but there's a very strong resemblance. I don't think I'd hesitate to say it's the same face."

He put the photo down on the desk and with the same unhurried motion took an automatic out of the drawer and put it down on the desk beside the photo.

Conant stared at the gun. His mouth twisted. He said thickly: "You won't need that, Senator. Listen, your showdown idea is all wrong. I'll get detailed confessions from these people and we'll hold them. If they ever act up again, it'll be time enough then to crack down with the big one."

Carmady smiled a little and walked across the carpet until he was near the end of the desk. He said: "I'd like to see that photograph" and leaned over suddenly and took it.

Courtway's thin hand dropped to the gun, then relaxed. He leaned back in his chair and stared at Carmady.

Carmady stared at the photograph, lowered it, said softly to Jean Adrian: "Go sit down."

She turned and went back to her chair, dropped into it wearily.

Carmady said: "I like your showdown idea, Senator. It's clean and straightforward and a wholesome change in policy from Mr. Conant. But it won't work." He snicked a fingernail at the photo. "This has a superficial resemblance, no more. I don't think it's the same girl at all myself. Her ears are differently shaped and lower on her head. Her eyes are closer together than Miss Adrian's eyes, the line of her jaw is longer. Those things don't change. So what have you got? An extortion letter. Maybe, but you can't tie it to anyone or you'd have done it already. The girl's name. Just coincidence. What else?"

Conant's face was granite hard, his mouth bitter. His voice shook a little saying: "And how about that certificate the gal took out of her purse, wise guy?"

Carmady smiled faintly, rubbed the side of his jaw with his fingertips. "I thought you got that from Shenvair?" he said slyly. "And Shenvair is dead."

Conant's face was a mask of fury. He balled his fist, took a jerky step forward. "Why you—damn louse—"

Jean Adrian was leaning forward staring round-eyed at Carmady. Targo was staring at him, with a loose grin, pale hard eyes. Courtway was staring at him. There was no expression of any kind on Courtway's face. He sat cold, relaxed, distant.

Conant laughed suddenly, snapped his fingers. "Okey, toot your horn," he grunted.

Carmady said slowly: "I'll tell you another reason why there'll be no showdown. That shooting at Cyrano's. Those threats to make Targo drop an unimportant fight. That hood that went to Miss Adrian's hotel room and sapped her, left her lying on her doorway. Can't you tie all that in, Conant? I can."

Courtway leaned forward suddenly and placed his hand on his gun, folded it around the butt. His black eyes were holes in a white frozen face.

Conant didn't move, didn't speak.

Carmady went on: "Why did Targo get those threats, and after he didn't drop the fight, why did a gun go to see him at Cyrano's, a night club, a very bad place for that kind of play? Because at Cyrano's he was with the girl, and Cyrano was his backer, and if anything happened at Cyrano's the law would get the threat story before they had time to think of anything else. That's why. The threats were a build-up for a killing. When the shooting came off Targo was to be with the girl, so the hood could get the girl and it would look as if Targo was the one he was after.

"He would have tried for Targo, too, of course, but above all he would have got the girl. Because she was the dynamite behind this shakedown, without her it meant nothing, and with her it could always be made over into a legitimate paternity suit. If it didn't work the other way. You know about her and about Targo, because Shenvair got cold feet and sold out. And Shenvair knew about the hood—because when the hood showed, and I saw him—and Shenvair knew I knew him, because he had heard me tell Targo about him—then Shenvair tried to pick a drunken fight with me and keep me from trying to interfere."

Carmady stopped, rubbed the side of his head again, very slowly, very gently. He watched Conant with an up-from-under look.

Conant said slowly, very harshly: "I don't play those games, buddy. Believe it or not—I don't."

Carmady said: "Listen. The hood could have killed the girl at the hotel with his sap. He didn't because Targo wasn't there and the fight hadn't been fought, and the build-up would have been all wasted. He went there to have a close look at her, without make-up. And she was scared about something, and had a gun with her. So he sapped her down and ran away. That visit was just a finger."

Conant said again: "I don't play those games, buddy." Then he took the Luger out of his pocket and held it down at his side.

Carmady shrugged, turned his head to stare at Senator Courtway.

"No, but he does," he said softly. "He had the motive, and the play wouldn't look like him. He cooked it up with Shenvair—and if it went wrong, as it did, Shenvair would have breezed and if the law got wise, big tough Doll Conant is the boy whose nose would be in the mud."

Courtway smiled a little and said in an utterly dead voice: "The young man is very ingenious, but surely—"

Targo stood up. His face was a stiff mask. His lips moved slowly and he said: "It sounds pretty good to

me. I think I'll twist your goddamn neck, Mister Courtway."

The albino snarled, "Sit down, punk," and lifted his
gun. Targo turned slightly and slammed the albino on
the jaw. He went over backwards, smashed his head
against the wall. The gun sailed along the floor from his
limp hand.

Targo started across the room.

Conant looked at him sidewise and didn't move.
Targo went past him, almost touching him. Conant
didn't move a muscle. His big face was blank, his eyes
narrowed to a faint glitter between the heavy lids.

Nobody moved but Targo. Then Courtway lifted his
gun and his finger whitened on the trigger and the gun
roared.

Carmady moved across the room very swiftly and
stood in front of Jean Adrian, between her and the rest
of the room.

Targo looked down at his hands. His face twisted
into a silly smile. He sat down on the floor and pressed
both his hands against his chest.

Courtway lifted his gun again and then Conant
moved. The Luger jerked up, flamed twice. Blood
flowed down Courtway's hand. His gun fell behind his
desk. His long body seemed to swoop down after the
gun. It jackknifed until only his shoulders showed
humped above the line of the desk.

Conant said: "Stand up and take it, you goddamn
double-crossing swine!"

There was a shot behind the desk. Courtway's shoulders went down out of sight.

After a moment Conant went around behind the
desk, stopped, straightened.

"He ate one," he said very calmly. "Through the
mouth . . . And I lose me a nice clean senator."

Targo took his hands from his chest and fell over
sidewise on the floor and lay still.

The door of the room slammed open. The butler

stood in it, tousle-headed, his mouth gaping. He tried to say something, saw the gun in Conant's hand, saw Targo slumped on the floor. He didn't say anything.

The albino was getting to his feet, rubbing his chin, feeling his teeth, shaking his head. He went slowly along the wall and gathered up his gun.

Conant snarled at him: "Swell gut you turned out to be. Get on the phone. Get Malloy, the night captain— and snap it up!"

Carmady turned, put his hand down and lifted Jean Adrian's cold chin.

"It's getting light, angel. And I think the rain has stopped," he said slowly. He pulled his inevitable flask out. "Let's take a drink—to Mister Targo."

The girl shook her head, covered her face with her hands.

After a long time there were sirens.

## 10

The slim, tired-looking kid in the pale and silver of the Carondelet held his white glove in front of the closing doors and said: "Corky's boils is better, but he didn't come to work, Mister Carmady. Tony the bell captain ain't showed this morning neither. Pretty soft for some guys."

Carmady stood close to Jean Adrian in the corner of the car. They were alone in it. He said: "That's what you think."

The boy turned red. Carmady moved over and patted his shoulder, said: "Don't mind me, son. I've been up all night with a sick friend. Here, buy yourself a second breakfast."

"Jeeze, Mister Carmady, I didn't mean—"

The doors opened at nine and they went down the corridor to 914. Carmady took the key and opened the door, put the key on the inside, held the door, said:

"Get some sleep and wake up with your fist in your eye. Take my flask and get a mild toot on. Do you good."

The girl went in through the door, said over her shoulder: "I don't want liquor. Come in a minute. There's something I want to tell you."

He shut the door and followed her in. A bright bar of sunlight lay across the carpet all the way to the davenport. He lit a cigarette and stared at it.

Jean Adrian sat down and jerked her hat off and rumpled her hair. She was silent a moment, then she said slowly, carefully: "It was swell of you to go to all that trouble for me. I don't know why you should do it."

Carmady said: "I can think of a couple of reasons, but they didn't keep Targo from getting killed, and that was my fault in a way. Then in another way it wasn't. I didn't ask him to twist Senator Courtway's neck."

The girl said: "You think you're hard-boiled but you're just a big slob that argues himself into a jam for the first tramp he finds in trouble. Forget it. Forget Targo and forget me. Neither of us was worth any part of your time. I wanted to tell you that because I'll be going away as soon as they let me, and I won't be seeing you any more. This is goodbye."

Carmady nodded, stared at the sun on the carpet. The girl went on: "It's a little hard to tell. I'm not looking for sympathy when I say I'm a tramp. I've smothered in too many hall bedrooms, stripped in too many filthy dressing rooms, missed too many meals, told too many lies to be anything else. That's why I wouldn't want to have anything to do with you, ever."

Carmady said: "I like the way you tell it. Go on."

She looked at him quickly, looked away again. "I'm not the Gianni girl. You guessed that. But I knew her. We did a cheap sister act together when they still did sister acts. Ada and Jean Adrian. We made up our names from hers. That flopped, and we went in a road show and that flopped too. In New Orleans. The going was a little too rough for her. She swallowed bichloride. I kept her photos because I knew her story. And looking at that thin cold guy and thinking what he could have done for her I got to hate him. She was his kid all right. Don't ever think she wasn't. I even wrote letters to him, asking for help for her, just a little help, signing her name. But they didn't get any answer. I got to hate him so much I wanted to do something to him, after she took the bichloride. So I came out here when I got a stake."

She stopped talking and laced her fingers together tightly, then pulled them apart violently, as if she wanted to hurt herself. She went on: "I met Targo through Cyrano and Shenvair through him. Shenvair knew the photos. He'd worked once for an agency in Frisco that was hired to watch Ada. You know all the rest of it."

Carmady said: "It sounds pretty good. I wondered why the touch wasn't made sooner. Do you want me to think you didn't want his money?"

"No. I'd have taken his money all right. But that wasn't what I wanted most. I said I was a tramp."

Carmady smiled very faintly and said: "You don't know a lot about tramps, angel. You made an illegitimate pass and you got caught. That's that, but the money wouldn't have done you any good. It would have been dirty money. I know."

She looked up at him, stared at him. He touched the side of his face and winced and said: "I know because that's the kind of money mine is. My dad made it out of crooked sewerage and paving contracts, out of gambling concessions, appointment pay-offs, even vice, I daresay. He made it every rotten way there is to make money in city politics. And when it was made and there was nothing left to do but sit and look at it, he died and left it to me. It hasn't brought me any fun either. I always hope it's going to, but it never does. Because I'm his pup, his blood, reared in the same gutter. I'm worse than a tramp, angel. I'm a guy that lives on crooked dough and doesn't even do his own stealing."

He stopped, flicked ash on the carpet, straightened his hat on his head.

"Think that over, and don't run too far, because I have all the time in the world and it wouldn't do you any good. It would be so much more fun to run away together."

He went a little way towards the door, stood looking down at the sunlight on the carpet, looked back at her quickly and then went on out.

When the door shut she stood up and went into the bedroom and lay down on the bed just as she was, with her coat on, She stared at the ceiling. After a long time she smiled. In the middle of the smile she fell asleep.

# NEVADA GAS

HUGO CANDLESS stood in the middle of the squash court bending his big body at the waist, holding the little black ball delicately between left thumb and forefinger. He dropped it near the service line and flicked at it with the long-handled racket.

The black ball hit the front wall a little less than halfway up, floated back in a high, lazy curve, skimmed just below the white ceiling and the lights behind wire protectors. It slid languidly down the back wall, never touching it enough to bounce out.

George Dial made a careless swing at it, whanged the end of his racket against the cement back wall. The ball fell dead.

He said: "That's the story, chief. 12—14. You're just too good for me."

George Dial was tall, dark, handsome, Hollywoodish. He was brown and lean, and had a hard, outdoor look. Everything about him was hard except his full, soft lips and his large, cowlike eyes.

"Yeah. I always was too good for you," Hugo Candless chortled.

He leaned far back from his thick waist and laughed with his mouth wide open. Sweat glistened on his chest and belly. He was naked except for blue shorts, white wool socks and heavy sneakers with crêpe soles. He had gray hair and a broad moon face with a small nose and mouth, sharp twinkly eyes.

"Want another lickin'?" he asked.

"Not unless I have to."

Hugo Candless scowled. "Oke," he said shortly. He stuck his racket under his arm and got an oilskin pouch out of his shorts, took a cigarette and a match from it. He lit the cigarette with a flourish and threw the match into the middle of the court, where somebody else would have to pick it up.

He threw the door of the squash court open and paraded down the corridor to the locker room with his chest out. Dial walked behind him silently; catlike, soft-footed, with a lithe grace. They went to the showers.

Candless sang in the showers, covered his big body with thick suds, showered dead-cold after the hot, and liked it. He rubbed himself dry with immense leisure, took another towel and stalked out of the shower room yelling for the attendant to bring ice and ginger ale.

A Negro in a stiff white coat came hurrying with a tray. Candless signed the check with a flourish, unlocked his big double locker and planked a bottle of Johnny Walker on the round green table that stood in the locker aisle.

The attendant mixed drinks carefully, two of them, said: "Yes, suh, Mista Candless," and went away palming a quarter.

George Dial, already fully dressed in smart gray flannels, came around the corner and lifted one of the drinks.

"Through for the day, chief?" He looked at the ceiling light through his drink, with tight eyes.

"Guess so," Candless said largely. "Guess I'll go home and give the little woman a treat." He gave Dial a swift, sidewise glance from his little eyes.

"Mind if I don't ride home with you?" Dial asked carelessly.

"With me it's okey. It's tough on Naomi," Candless said unpleasantly.

Dial made a soft sound with his lips, shrugged, said: "You like to burn people up, don't you chief?"

Candless didn't answer, didn't look at him. Dial stood silent with his drink and watched the big man put on monogrammed satin underclothes, purple socks with gray clocks, a monogrammed silk shirt, a suit of tiny black and white checks that made him look as big as a barn.

By the time he got to his purple tie he was yelling for the Negro to come and mix another drink.

Dial refused the second drink, nodded, went away softly along the matting between the tall green lockers.

Candless finished dressing, drank his second highball, locked his liquor away and put a fat brown cigar in his mouth. He had the Negro light the cigar for him. He went off with a strut and several loud greetings here and there.

It seemed very quiet in the locker room after he went out. There were a few snickers.


It was raining outside the Delmar Club. The liveried doorman helped Hugo Candless on with his belted white slicker and went out for his car. When he had it in front of the canopy he held an umbrella over Hugo across the strip of wooden matting to the curb. The car was a royal blue Lincoln limousine, with buff striping. The license number was 5A6.

The chauffeur, in a black slicker turned up high around his ears, didn't look around. The doorman opened the door and Hugo Candless got in and sank heavily on the back seat.

" 'Night, Sam. Tell him to go on home."

The doorman touched his cap, shut the door, and relayed the orders to the driver, who nodded without turning his head. The car moved off in the rain.

The rain came down slantingly and at the intersection sudden gusts blew it rattling against the glass of the limousine. The street corners were clotted with people trying to get across Sunset without being splashed. Hugo Candless grinned out at them, pityingly.

The car went out Sunset, through Sherman, then swung towards the hills. It began to go very fast. It was on a boulevard where traffic was thin now.

It was very hot in the car. The windows were all shut and the glass partition behind the driver's seat was shut all the way across. The smoke of Hugo's cigar was heavy and choking in the tonneau of the limousine.

Candless scowled and reached out to lower a window. The window lever didn't work. He tried the other side. That didn't work either. He began to get mad. He grabbed for the little telephone dingus to bawl his driver out. There wasn't any little telephone dingus.

The car turned sharply and began to go up a long straight hill with eucalyptus trees on one side and no houses. Candless felt something cold touch his spine, all the way up and down his spine. He bent forward and banged on the glass with his fist. The driver didn't turn his head. The car went very fast up the long dark hill road.

Hugo Candless grabbed viciously for the door handle. The doors didn't have any handles—either side. A sick, incredulous grin broke over Hugo's broad moon face.

The driver bent over to the right and reached for something with his gloved hand. There was a sudden sharp hissing noise. Hugo Candless began to smell the odor of almonds.

Very faint at first—very faint, and rather pleasant. The hissing noise went on. The smell of almonds got bitter and harsh and very deadly. Hugo Candless dropped his cigar and banged with all his strength on the glass of the nearest window. The glass didn't break.

The car was up in the hills now, beyond even the infrequent street lights of the residential sections.

Candless dropped back on the seat and lifted his foot to kick hard at the glass partition in front of him. The kick was never finished. His eyes no longer saw. His face twisted into a snarl and his head went back against the cushions, crushed down against his thick shoulders. His soft white felt hat was shapeless on his big square skull.

The driver looked back quickly, showing a lean, hawklike face for a brief instant. Then he bent to his right again and the hissing noise stopped.

He pulled over to the side of the deserted road, stopped the car, switched off all the lights. The rain made a dull noise pounding on the roof.

The driver got out in the rain and opened the rear door of the car, then backed away from it quickly, holding his nose.

He stood a little way off for a while and looked up and down the road.

In the back of the limousine Hugo Candless didn't move.

## 2

Francine Ley sat in a low red chair beside a small table on which there was an alabaster bowl. Smoke from the cigarette she had just discarded into the bowl floated up and made patterns in the still, warm air. Her hands were clasped behind her head and her smoke-blue eyes were lazy, inviting. She had dark auburn hair set in loose waves. There were bluish shadows in the troughs of the waves.

George Dial leaned over and kissed her on the lips, hard. His own lips were hot when he kissed her, and he shivered. The girl didn't move. She smiled up at him lazily when he straightened again.

In a thick, clogged voice Dial said: "Listen, Francy.

When do you ditch this gambler and let me set you up?"

Francine Ley shrugged, without taking her hands from behind her head. "He's a square gambler, George," she drawled. "That's something nowadays and you don't have enough money."

"I can get it."

"How?" Her voice was low and husky. It moved George Dial like a cello.

"From Candless. I've got plenty on that bird."

"As for instance?" Francine Ley suggested lazily.

Dial grinned softly down at her. He widened his eyes in a deliberately innocent expression. Francine Ley thought the whites of his eyes were tinged ever so faintly with some color that was not white.

Dial flourished an unlighted cigarette. "Plenty—like he sold out a tough boy from Reno last year. The tough boy's half-brother was under a murder rap here and Candless took twenty-five grand to get him off. He made a deal with the D.A. on another case and let the tough boy's brother go up."

"And what did the tough boy do about all that?" Francine Ley asked gently.

"Nothing—yet. He thinks it was on the up and up, I guess. You can't always win."

"But he might do plenty, if he knew." Francine Ley said, nodding. "Who was the tough boy, Georgie?"

Dial lowered his voice and leaned down over her again. "I'm a sap to tell you that. A man named Zapparty. I've never met him."

"And never want to—if you've got sense, Georgie. No, thanks. I'm not walking myself into any jam like that with you."

Dial smiled lightly, showing even teeth in a dark, smooth face. "Leave it to me, Francy. Just forget the whole thing except how I'm nuts about you."

"Buy us a drink," the girl said.

The room was a living room in a hotel apartment. It

was all red and white, with embassy decorations, too stiff. The white walls had red designs painted on them, the white venetian blinds were framed in white box drapes, there was a half-round red rug with a white border in front of the gas fire. There was a kidney-shaped white desk against one wall, between the windows.

Dial went over to the desk and poured Scotch into two glasses, added ice and charged water, carried the glasses back across the room to where a thin wisp of smoke still plumed upward from the alabaster bowl.

"Ditch the gambler," Dial said, handing her a glass. "He's the one will get you in a jam."

She sipped the drink, nodded. Dial took the glass out of her hand, sipped from the same place on the rim, leaned over holding both glasses and kissed her on the lips again.

There were red curtains over a door to a short hallway. They were parted a few inches and a man's face appeared in the opening, cool gray eyes stared in thoughtfully at the kiss. The curtains fell together again without sound.

After a moment a door shut loudly and steps came along the hallway. Johnny De Ruse came through the curtains into the room. By that time Dial was lighting his cigarette.

Johnny De Ruse was tall, lean, quiet, dressed in dark clothes dashingly cut. His cool gray eyes had fine laughter wrinkles at the corners. His thin mouth was delicate but not soft, and his long chin had a cleft in it.

Dial stared at him, made a vague motion with his hand. De Ruse walked over to the desk without speaking, poured some whiskey into a glass and drank it straight.

He stood a moment with his back to the room, tapping on the edge of the desk. Then he turned around, smiled faintly, said: " 'Lo, people," in a gentle, rather drawling voice and went out of the room through an inner door.

He was in a big overdecorated bedroom with twin beds. He went to a closet and got a tan calfskin suitcase out of it, opened it on the nearest bed. He began to rob the drawers of a highboy and put things in the suitcase, arranging them carefully, without haste. He whistled quietly through his teeth while he was doing it.

When the suitcase was packed he snapped it shut and lit a cigarette. He stood for a moment in the middle of the room without moving. His gray eyes looked at the wall without seeing it.

After a little while he went back into the closet and came out with a small gun in a soft leather harness with two short straps. He pulled up the left leg of his trousers and strapped the holster on his leg. Then he picked up the suitcase and went back to the living room.

Francine Ley's eyes narrowed swiftly when she saw the suitcase.

"Going some place?" she asked in her low, husky voice.

"Uh-huh. Where's Dial?"

"He had to leave."

"That's too bad," De Ruse said softly. He put the suitcase down on the floor and stood beside it, moving his cool gray eyes over the girl's face, up and down her slim body, from her ankles to her auburn head. "That's too bad," he said. "I like to see him around. I'm kind of dull for you."

"Maybe you are, Johnny."

He bent to the suitcase, but straightened without touching it and said casually: "Remember Mops Parisi? I saw him in town today."

Her eyes widened and then almost shut. Her teeth clicked lightly. The line of her jawbone stood out very distinctly for a moment.

De Ruse kept moving his glance up and down her face and body.

"Going to do anything about it?" she asked.

"I thought of taking a trip," De Ruse said. "I'm not so scrappy as I was once."

"A powder," Francine Ley said softly. "Where do we go?"

"Not a powder—a trip," De Ruse said tonelessly. "And not we—*me*. I'm going alone."

She sat still, watching his face, not moving a muscle.

De Ruse reached inside his coat and got out a long wallet that opened like a book. He tossed a tight sheaf of bills into the girl's lap, put the wallet away. She didn't touch the bills.

"That'll hold you for longer than you'll need to find a new playmate," he said, without expression. "I wouldn't say I won't send you more, if you need it."

She stood up slowly and the sheaf of bills slid down her skirt to the floor. She held her arms straight down at the sides, the hands clenched so that the tendons on the backs of them were sharp. Her eyes were as dull as slate.

"That means we're through, Johnny?"

He lifted his suitcase. She stepped in front of him swiftly, with two long steps. She put a hand against his coat. He stood quite still, smiling gently with his eyes, but not with his lips. The perfume of Shalimar twitched at his nostrils.

"You know what you are, Johnny?" Her husky voice was almost a lisp.

He waited.

"A pigeon, Johnny. A pigeon."

He nodded slightly. "Check. I called copper on Mops Parisi. I don't like the snatch racket, baby. I'd call copper on it any day. I might even get myself hurt blocking it. That's old stuff. Through?"

"You called copper on Mops Parisi and you don't think he knows it, but maybe he does. So you're running away from him . . . That's a laugh, Johnny. I'm kidding you. That's not why you're leaving me."

"Maybe I'm just tired of you, baby."

She put her head back and laughed sharply, almost with a wild note. De Ruse didn't budge.

"You're not a tough boy, Johnny. You're soft. George Dial is harder than you are. Gawd, how soft you are, Johnny!"

She stepped back, staring at his face. Some flicker of almost unbearable emotion came and went in her eyes.

"You're such a handsome pup, Johnny. Gawd, but you're handsome. It's too bad you're soft."

De Ruse said gently, without moving: "Not soft, baby—just a bit sentimental. I like to clock the ponies and play seven-card stud and mess around with little red cubes with white spots on them. I like games of chance, including women. But when I lose I don't get sore and I don't chisel. I just move on to the next table. Be seein' you."

He stooped, hefted the suitcase, and walked around her. He went across the room and through the red curtains without looking back.

Francine Ley stared with stiff eyes at the floor.

### 3

Standing under the scalloped glass canopy of the side entrance to the Chatterton, De Ruse looked up and down Irolo, towards the flashing lights of Wilshire and towards the dark quiet end of the side street.

The rain fell softly, slantingly. A light drop blew in under the canopy and hit the red end of his cigarette with a sputter. He hefted the suitcase and went along Irolo towards his sedan. It was parked almost at the next corner, a shiny black Packard with a little discreet chromium here and there.

He stopped and opened the door and a gun came up swiftly from inside the car. The gun prodded against his chest. A voice said sharply: "Hold it! The mitts high, sweets!"

De Ruse saw the man dimly inside the car. A lean hawklike face on which some reflected light fell without making it distinct. He felt a gun hard against his chest, hurting his breastbone. Quick steps came up behind him and another gun prodded his back.

"Satisfied?" another voice inquired.

De Ruse dropped the suitcase, lifted his hands and put them against the top of the car.

"Okey," he said wearily. "What is it—a heist?"

A snarling laugh came from the man in the car. A hand smacked De Ruse's hips from behind.

"Back up—slow!"

De Ruse backed up, holding his hands very high in the air.

"Not so high, punk," the man behind said dangerously. "Just shoulder high."

De Ruse lowered them. The man in the car got out, straightened. He put his gun against De Ruse's chest again, put out a long arm and unbuttoned De Ruse's overcoat. De Ruse leaned backwards. The hand belonging to the long arm explored his pockets, his armpits. A .38 in a spring holster ceased to make weight under his arm.

"Got one, Chuck. Anything your side?"

"Nothin' on the hip."

The man in front stepped away and picked up the suitcase.

"March sweets. We'll ride in our heap."

They went farther along Irolo. A big Lincoln limousine loomed up, a blue car with a lighter stripe. The hawk-faced man opened the rear door.

"In."

De Ruse got in listlessly, spitting his cigarette end into the wet darkness, as he stooped under the roof of the car. A faint smell assailed his nose, a smell that might have been overripe peaches or almonds. He got into the car.

"In beside him, Chuck."

"Listen. Let's all ride up front. I can handle——"

"Nix. In beside him, Chuck," the hawk-faced one snapped.

Chuck growled, got into the back seat beside De Ruse. The other man slammed the door hard. His lean face showed through the closed window in a sardonic grin. Then he went around to the driver's seat and started the car, tooled it away from the curb.

DeRuse wrinkled his nose, sniffing at the queer smell.

They spun at the corner, went east on Eighth to Normandie, north on Normandie across Wilshire, across other streets, up over a steep hill and down the other side to Melrose. The big Lincoln slid through the light rain without a whisper. Chuck sat in the corner, held his gun on his knee, scowled. Street lights showed a square, arrogant red face, a face that was not at ease.

The back of the driver's head was motionless beyond the glass partition. They passed Sunset and Hollywood, turned east on Franklin, swung north to Los Feliz and down Los Feliz towards the river bed.

Cars coming up the hill threw sudden brief glares of white light into the interior of the Lincoln. De Ruse tensed, waited. At the next pair of lights that shot squarely into the car he bent over swiftly and jerked up the left leg of his trousers. He was back against the cushions before the blinding light was gone.

Chuck hadn't moved, hadn't noticed movement.

Down at the bottom of the hill, at the intersection of Riverside Drive, a whole phalanx of cars surged towards them as a light changed. De Ruse waited, timed the impact of the headlights. His body stooped briefly, his hand swooped down, snatched the small gun from the leg holster.

He leaned back once more, the gun against the bulk

of his left thigh, concealed behind it from where Chuck sat.

The Lincoln shot over on to Riverside and passed the entrance to Griffith Park.

"Where we going, punk?" De Ruse asked casually.

"Save it," Chuck snarled. "You'll find out."

"Not a stick-up, huh?"

"Save it," Chuck snarled again.

"Mops Parisi's boys?" De Ruse asked thinly, slowly.

The red-faced gunman jerked, lifted the gun off his knee. "I said—save it!"

De Ruse said: "Sorry, punk."

He turned the gun over his thigh, lined it swiftly, squeezed the trigger left-handed. The gun made a small flat sound—almost an unimportant sound.

Chuck yelled and his hand jerked wildly. The gun kicked out of it and fell on the floor of the car. His left hand raced for his right shoulder.

De Ruse shifted the little Mauser to his right hand and put it deep into Chuck's side.

"Steady, boy, steady. Keep your hands out of trouble. Now—kick that cannon over this way—fast!"

Chuck kicked the big automatic along the floor of the car. De Ruse reached down for it swiftly, got it. The lean-faced driver jerked a look back and the car swerved, then straightened again.

De Ruse hefted the big gun. The Mauser was too light for a sap. He slammed Chuck hard on the side of the head. Chuck groaned, sagged forward, clawing.

"The gas!" he bleated. "The gas! He'll turn on the gas!"

De Ruse hit him again, harder. Chuck was a tumbled heap on the floor of the car.

The Lincoln swung off Riverside, over a short bridge and a bridle path, down a narrow dirt road that split a golf course. It went into darkness and among trees. It went fast, rocketed from side to side, as if the driver wanted it to do just that.

De Ruse steadied himself, felt for the door handle. There wasn't any door handle. His lips curled and he smashed at a window with the gun. The heavy glass was like a wall of stone.

The hawk-faced man leaned over and there was a hissing sound. Then there was a sudden sharp increase of intensity of the smell of almonds.

De Ruse tore a handkerchief out of his pocket and pressed it to his nose. The driver had straightened again now and was driving hunched over, trying to keep his head down.

De Ruse held the muzzle of the big gun close to the glass partition behind the driver's head, who ducked sidewise. He squeezed lead four times quickly, shutting his eyes and turning his head away, like a nervous woman.

No glass flew. When he looked again there was a jagged round hole in the glass and the windshield in a line with it was starred but not broken.

He slammed the gun at the edges of the hole and managed to knock a piece of glass loose. He was getting the gas now, through the handkerchief. His head felt like a balloon. His vision waved and wandered.

The hawk-faced driver, crouched, wrenched the door open at his side, swung the wheel of the car the opposite way and jumped clear.

The car tore over a low embankment, looped a little and smacked sidewise against a tree. The body twisted enough for one of the rear doors to spring open.

De Ruse went through the door in a headlong dive. Soft earth smacked him, knocked some of the wind out of him. Then his lungs breathed clean air. He rolled up on his stomach and elbows, kept his head down, his gun hand up.

The hawk-faced man was on his knees a dozen yards away. De Ruse watched him drag a gun out of his pocket and lift it.

Chucks' gun pulsed and roared in De Ruse's hand until it was empty.

The hawk-faced man folded down slowly and his body merged with the dark shadows and the wet ground. Cars went by distantly on Riverside Drive. Rain dripped off the trees. The Griffith Park beacon turned in the thick sky. The rest was darkness and silence.

De Ruse took a deep breath and got up on his feet. He dropped the empty gun, took a small flash out of his overcoat pocket and pulled his overcoat up against his nose and mouth, pressing the thick cloth hard against his face. He went to the car, switched off the lights and threw the beam of the flash into the driver's compartment. He leaned in quickly and turned a petcock on a copper cylinder like a fire extinguisher. The hissing noise of the gas stopped.

He went over to the hawk-faced man. He was dead. There was some loose money, currency and silver in his pockets, cigarettes, a folder of matches from the Club Egypt, no wallet, a couple of extra clips of cartridges, De Ruse's .38. De Ruse put the last back where it belonged and straightened from the sprawled body.

He looked across the darkness of the Los Angeles river bed towards the lights of Glendale. In the middle distance a green neon sign far from any other light winked on and off: Club Egypt.

De Ruse smiled quietly to himself, and went back to the Lincoln. He dragged Chuck's body out onto the wet ground. Chuck's red face was blue now, under the beam of the small flash. His open eyes held an empty stare. His chest didn't move. De Ruse put the flash down and went through some more pockets.

He found the usual things a man carries, including a wallet showing a driver's license issued to Charles Le Grand, Hotel Metropole, Los Angeles. He found more Club Egypt matches and a tabbed hotel key marked 809, Hotel Metropole.

He put the key in his pocket, slammed the sprung door of the Lincoln, got in under the wheel. The motor caught. He backed the car away from the tree with a wrench of broken fender metal, swung it around slowly over the soft earth and got it back again on the road.

When he reached Riverside again he turned the lights on and drove back to Hollywood. He put the car under some pepper trees in front of a big brick apartment house on Kenmore half a block north of Hollywood Boulevard, locked the ignition and lifted out his suitcase.

Light from the entrance of the apartment house rested on the front license plate as he walked away. He wondered why gunmen would use a car with plate numbers reading 5A6, almost a privilege number.

In a drugstore he phoned for a taxi. The taxi took him back to the Chatterton.

## 4

The apartment was empty. The smell of Shalimar and cigarette smoke lingered on the warm air, as if someone had been there not long before. De Ruse pushed into the bedroom, looked at clothes in two closets, articles on a dresser, then went back to the red and white living room and mixed himself a stiff highball.

He put the night latch on the outside door and carried his drink into the bedroom, stripped off his muddy clothes and put on another suit of somber material but dandified cut. He sipped his drink while he knotted a black four-in-hand in the opening of a soft white linen shirt.

He swabbed the barrel of the little Mauser, reassembled it, and added a shell to the small clip, slipped the gun back into the leg holster. Then he washed his hands and took his drink to the telephone.

The first number he called was the *Chronicle*. He asked for the City Room, Werner.

A drawly voice dripped over the wire: "Werner talkin'. Go ahead. Kid me."

De Ruse said: "This is John De Ruse, Claude. Look up California License 5A6 on your list for me."

"Must be a bloody politician," the drawly voice said, and went away.

De Ruse sat motionless, looking at a fluted white pillar in the corner. It had a red and white bowl of red and white artificial roses on top of it. He wrinkled his nose at it disgustedly.

Werner's voice came back on the wire: "1930 Lincoln limousine registered to Hugo Candless, Casa de Oro Apartments, 2942 Clearwater Street, West Hollywood."

De Ruse said in a tone that meant nothing: "That's the mouthpiece, isn't it?"

"Yeah. The big lip. Mister Take the Witness." Werner's voice came down lower. "Speaking to you, Johnny, and not for publication—a big crooked tub of guts that's not even smart; just been around long enough to know who's for sale . . . Story in it?"

"Hell, no," De Ruse said softly. "He just sideswiped me and didn't stop."

He hung up and finished his drink, stood up to mix another. Then he swept a telephone directory onto the white desk and looked up the number of the Casa de Oro. He dialed it. A switchboard operator told him Mr. Hugo Candless was out of town.

"Give me his apartment," De Ruse said.

A woman's cool voice answered the phone. "Yes. This is Mrs. Hugo Candless speaking. What is it, please?"

De Ruse said: "I'm a client of Mr. Candless, very anxious to get hold of him. Can you help me?"

"I'm very sorry," the cool, almost lazy voice told him. "My husband was called out of town quite sud-

denly. I don't even know where he went, though I
expect to hear from him later this evening. He left his
club——"

"What club was that?" De Ruse asked casually.

"The Delmar Club. I say he left there without coming home. If there is any message—"

De Ruse said: "Thank you, Mrs. Candless. Perhaps I
may call you again later."

He hung up, smiled slowly and grimly, sipped his
fresh drink and looked up the number of the Hotel
Metropole. He called it and asked for "Mister Charles
Le Grand in Room 809."

"Six-o-nine," the operator said casually. "I'll connect
you." A moment later: "There is no answer."

De Ruse thanked her, took the tabbed key out of his
pocket, looked at the number on it. The number was
809.

## 5

Sam, the doorman at the Delmar Club, leaned against
the buff stone of the entrance and watched the traffic
swish by on Sunset Boulevard. The headlights hurt his
eyes. He was tired and he wanted to go home. He
wanted a smoke and a big slug of gin. He wished the
rain would stop. It was dead inside the club when it
rained.

He straightened away from the wall and walked the
length of the sidewalk canopy a couple of times, slap-
ping together his big black hands in big white gloves.
He tried to whistle the "Skaters Waltz," couldn't get
within a block of the tune, whistled "Low Down
Lady" instead. That didn't have any tune.

De Ruse came around the corner from Hudson
Street and stood beside him near the wall.

"Hugo Candless inside?" he asked, not looking at
Sam.

Sam clicked his teeth disapprovingly. "He ain't."

"Been in?"

"Ask at the desk 'side, please, mistah."

De Ruse took gloved hands out of his pocket and began to roll a five-dollar bill around his left forefinger.

"What do they know that you don't know?"

Sam grinned slowly, watched the bill being wound tightly around the gloved finger.

"That's a fac', boss. Yeah—he was in. Comes most every day."

"What time he leave?"

"He leave 'bout six-thirty, Ah reckon."

"Drive his blue Lincoln limousine?"

"Shuah. Only he don't drive it hisself. What for you ask?"

"It was raining then," De Ruse said calmly. "Raining pretty hard. Maybe it wasn't the Lincoln."

" 'Twas, too, the Lincoln," Sam protested. "Ain't I tucked him in? He never rides nothin' else."

"License 5A6?" De Ruse bored on relentlessly.

"That's it," Sam chortled. "Just like a councilman's number that number is."

"Know the driver?"

"Shuah—" Sam began, and then stopped cold. He raked a black jaw with a white finger the size of a banana. "Well, Ah'll be a big black slob if he ain't got hisself a new driver again. I ain't *know* that man, sure 'nough."

De Ruse poked the rolled bill into Sam's big white paw. Sam grabbed it but his large eyes suddenly got suspicious.

"Say, for what you ask all of them questions, mistah man?"

De Ruse said: "I paid my way, didn't I?"

He went back around the corner to Hudson and got into his black Packard sedan. He drove it out on to Sunset, then west on Sunset almost to Beverly Hills, then turned towards the foothills and began to peer at

the signs on street corners. Clearwater Street ran along
the flank of a hill and had a view of the entire city. The
Casa de Oro, at the corner of Parkinson, was a tricky
block of high-class bungalow apartments surrounded by
an adobe wall with red tiles on top. It had a lobby in a
separate building, a big private garage on Parkinson,
opposite one length of the wall.

De Ruse parked across the street from the garage
and sat looking through the wide window into a
glassed-in office where an attendant in spotless white
coveralls sat with his feet on the desk, reading a magazine and spit over his shoulder at an invisible cuspidor.

De Ruse got out of the Packard, crossed the street
farther up, came back and slipped into the garage
without the attendant seeing him.

The cars were in four rows. Two rows backed against
the white walls, two against each other in the middle.
There were plenty of vacant stalls, but plenty of cars
had gone to bed also. They were mostly big, expensive
closed models, with two or three flashy open jobs.

There was only one limousine. It had License No.
5A6.

It was a well-kept car, bright and shiny; royal blue
with a buff trimming. De Ruse took a glove off and
rested his hand on the radiator shell. Quite cold. He
felt the tires, looked at his fingers. A little fine dry dust
adhered to the skin. There was no mud in the treads,
just bone-dry dust.

He went back along the row of dark car bodies and
leaned in the open door of the little office. After a
moment the attendant looked up, almost with a start.

"Seen the Candless chauffeur around?" De Ruse
asked him.

The man shook his head and spat deftly into a
copper spittoon.

"Not since I came on—three o'clock."

"Didn't he go down to the club for the old man?"

"Nope. I guess not. The big hack ain't been out. He always takes that."

"Where does he hang his hat?"

"Who? Mattick? They got servants' quarters in back of the jungle. But I think I heard him say he parks at some hotel. Let's see—" A brow got furrowed.

"The Metropole?" De Ruse suggested.

The garage man thought it over while De Ruse stared at the point of his chin.

"Yeah. I think that's it. I ain't just positive though. Mattick don't open up much."

De Ruse thanked him and crossed the street and got into the Packard again. He drove downtown.

It was twenty-five minutes past nine when he got to the corner of Seventh and Spring, where the Metropole was.

It was an old hotel that had once been exclusive and was now steering a shaky course between a receivership and a bad name at Headquarters. It had too much oily dark wood paneling, too many chipped gilt mirrors. Too much smoke hung below its low beamed lobby ceiling and too many grifters bummed around in its worn leather rockers.

The blonde who looked after the big horseshoe cigar counter wasn't young any more and her eyes were cynical from standing off cheap dates. De Ruse leaned on the glass and pushed his hat back on his crisp black hair.

"Camels, honey," he said in his low-pitched gambler's voice.

The girl smacked the pack in front of him, rang up fifteen cents and slipped the dime change under his elbow, with a faint smile. Her eyes said they liked him. She leaned opposite him and put her head near enough so that he could smell the perfume in her hair.

"Tell me something," De Ruse said.

"What?" she asked softly.

"Find out who lives in eight-o-nine, without telling any answers to the clerk."

The blonde looked disappointed. "Why don't you ask him yourself, mister?"

"I'm too shy," De Ruse said.

"Yes you are!"

She went to her telephone and talked into it with languid grace, came back to De Ruse.

"Name of Mattick. Mean anything?"

"Guess not," De Ruse said. "Thanks a lot. How do you like it in this nice hotel?"

"Who said it was a nice hotel?"

De Ruse smiled, touched his hat, strolled away. Her eyes looked after him sadly. She leaned her sharp elbows on the counter and cupped her chin in her hands to stare after him.

De Ruse crossed the lobby and went up three steps and got into an open-cage elevator that started with a lurch.

"Eight," he said, and leaned against the cage with his hands in his pockets.

Eight was as high as the Metropole went. De Ruse followed a long corridor that smelled of varnish. A turn at the end brought him face to face with 809. He knocked on the dark wood panel. Nobody answered. He bent over, looked through an empty keyhole, knocked again.

Then he took the tabbed key out of his pocket and unlocked the door and went in.

Windows were shut in two walls. The air reeked of whiskey. Lights were on in the ceiling. There was a wide brass bed, a dark bureau, a couple of brown leather rockers, a stiff-looking desk with a flat brown quart of Four Roses on it, nearly empty, without a cap. De Ruse sniffed it and set his hips against the edge of the desk, let his eyes prowl the room.

His glance traversed from the dark bureau across the bed and the wall with the door in it to another door behind which light showed. He crossed to that and opened it.

The man lay on his face, on the yellowish brown woodstone floor of the bathroom. Blood on the floor looked sticky and black. Two soggy patches on the back of the man's head were the points from which rivulets of dark red had run down the side of his neck to the floor. The blood had stopped flowing a long time ago.

De Ruse slipped a glove off and stooped to hold two fingers against the place where an artery would beat. He shook his head and put his hand back into his glove.

He left the bathroom, shut the door and went to open one of the windows. He leaned out, breathing clean rain-wet air, looking down along slants of thin rain into the dark slit of an alley.

After a little while he shut the window again, switched off the light in the bathroom, took a "Do Not Disturb" sign out of the top bureau drawer, doused the ceiling lights, and went out.

He hung the sign on the knob and went back along the corridor to the elevators and left the Hotel Metropole.

## 6

Francine Ley hummed low down in her throat as she went along the silent corridor of the Chatterton. She hummed unsteadily without knowing what she was humming, and her left hand with its cherry-red fingernails held a green velvet cape from slipping down off her shoulders. There was a wrapped bottle under her other arm.

She unlocked the door, pushed it open and stopped, with a quick frown. She stood still, remembering, trying to remember. She was still a little tight.

She had left the lights on, that was it. They were off now. Could be the maid service, of course. She went on in, fumbled through the red curtains into the living room.

The glow from the heater prowled across the red and white rug and touched shiny black things with a ruddy gleam. The shiny black things were shoes. They didn't move.

Francine Ley said: "Oh—oh," in a sick voice. The hand holding the cape almost tore into her neck with its long, beautifully molded nails.

Something clicked and light glowed in a lamp beside an easy chair. De Ruse sat in the chair, looking at her woodenly.

He had his coat and hat on. His eyes shrouded, far away, filled with a remote brooding.

He said: "Been out, Francy?"

She sat down slowly on the edge of a half-round settee, put the bottle down beside her.

"I got tight," she said. "Thought I'd better eat. Then I thought I'd get tight again." She patted the bottle.

De Ruse said: "I think your friend Dial's boss has been snatched." He said it casually, as if it was of no importance to him.

Francine Ley opened her mouth slowly and as she opened it all the prettiness went out of her face. Her face became a blank haggard mask on which rouge burned violently. Her mouth looked as if it wanted to scream.

After a while it closed again and her face got pretty again and her voice, from far off, said: "Would it do any good to say I don't know what you're talking about?"

De Ruse didn't change his wooden expression. He said: "When I went down to the street from here a couple of hoods jumped me. One of them was stashed in the car. Of course they could have spotted me somewhere else—followed me here."

"They did," Francine Ley said breathlessly. "They did, Johnny."

His long chin moved an inch. "They piled me into a big Lincoln, a limousine. It was quite a car. It had heavy glass that didn't break easily and no door handles and it was all shut up tight. In the front seat it had a tank of Nevada gas, cyanide, which the guy driving could turn into the back part without getting it himself. They took me out Griffith Parkway, towards the Club Egypt. That's that joint on county land, near the airport." He paused, rubbed the end of one eyebrow, went on: "They overlooked the Mauser I sometimes wear on my leg. The driver crashed the car and I got loose."

He spread his hands and looked down at them. A faint metallic smile showed at the corners of his lips.

Francine Ley said: "I didn't have anything to do with it, Johnny." Her voice was as dead as the summer before last.

De Ruse said: "The guy that rode in the car before I did probably didn't have a gun. He was Hugo Candless. The car was a ringer for his car—same model, same paint job, same plates—but it wasn't his car. Somebody took a lot of trouble. Candless left the Delmar Club in the wrong car about six-thirty. His wife says he's out of town. I talked to her an hour ago. His car hasn't been out of the garage since noon . . . Maybe his wife knows he's snatched by now, maybe not."

Francine Ley's nails clawed at her skirt. Her lips shook.

De Ruse went on calmly, tonelessly: "Somebody gunned the Candless chauffeur in a downtown hotel tonight or this afternoon. The cops haven't found it yet. Somebody took a lot of trouble, Francy. You wouldn't want to be in on that kind of a set-up, would you, precious?"

Francine Ley bent her head forward and stared at the floor. She said thickly: "I need a drink. What I had is dying in me. I feel awful."

De Ruse stood up and went to the white desk. He drained a bottle into a glass and brought it across to her. He stood in front of her, holding the glass out of her reach.

"I only get tough once in a while, baby, but when I get tough I'm not so easy to stop, if I say it myself. If you know anything about all this, now would be a good time to spill it."

He handed her the glass. She gulped the whiskey and a little more light came into her smoke-blue eyes. She said slowly: "I don't know anything about it, Johnny. Not in the way you mean. But George Dial made me a love-nest proposition tonight and he told me he could get money out of Candless by threatening to spill a dirty trick Candless played on some tough boy from Reno."

"Damn clever, these greasers," De Ruse said. "Reno's my town, baby. I know all the tough boys in Reno. Who was it?"

"Somebody named Zapparty."

De Ruse said very softly: "Zapparty is the name of the man who runs the Club Egypt."

Francine Ley stood up suddenly and grabbed his arm. "Stay out of it, Johnny! For Christ sake, can't you stay out of it for just this once?"

De Ruse shook his head, smiled delicately, lingeringly at her. Then he lifted her hand off his arm and stepped back.

"I had a ride in their gas car, baby, and I didn't like it. I smelled their Nevada gas. I left my lead in somebody's gun punk. That makes me call copper or get jammed up with the law. If somebody's snatched and I call copper, there'll be another kidnap victim bumped off, more likely than not. Zapparty's a tough boy from Reno and that could tie in with what Dial told you, and if Mops Parisi is playing with Zapparty, that could make a reason to pull me into it. Parisi loathes my guts."

"You don't have to be a one-man riot squad, Johnny," Francine Ley said desperately.

He kept on smiling, with tight lips and solemn eyes. "There'll be two of us, baby. Get yourself a long coat. It's still raining a little."

She goggled at him. Her outstretched hand, the one that had been on his arm, spread its fingers stiffly, bent back from the palm, straining back. Her voice was hollow with fear.

"Me, Johnny? . . . Oh, please, not . . ."

De Ruse said gently: "Get that coat, honey. Make yourself look nice. It might be the last time we'll go out together."

She staggered past him. He touched her arm softly, held it a moment, said almost in a whisper:

"*You* didn't put the finger on me, did you, Francy?"

She looked back stonily at the pain in his eyes, made a hoarse sound under her breath and jerked her arm loose, went quickly into the bedroom.

After a moment the pain went out of De Ruse's eyes and the metallic smile came back to the corners of his lips.

## 7

De Ruse half closed his eyes and watched the croupier's fingers as they slid back across the table and rested on the edge. They were round, plump, tapering fingers, graceful fingers. De Ruse raised his head and looked at the croupier's face. He was a bald-headed man of no particular age, with quiet blue eyes. He had no hair on his head at all, not a single hair.

De Ruse looked down at the croupier's hands again. The right hand turned a little on the edge of the table. The buttons on the sleeve of the croupier's brown velvet coat—cut like a dinner coat—rested on the edge of the table. De Ruse smiled his thin metallic smile.

He had three blue chips on the red. On that play the ball stopped at Black 2. The croupier paid off two of the four other men who were playing.

De Ruse pushed five blue chips forward and settled them on the red diamond. Then he turned his head to the left and watched a huskily built blond young man put three red chips on the zero.

De Ruse licked his lips and turned his head farther, looked towards the side of the rather small room. Francine Ley was sitting on a couch backed to the wall, with ther head leaning against it.

"I think I've got it, baby," De Ruse said to her. "I think I've got it."

Francine Ley blinked and lifted her head away from the wall. She reached for a drink on a low round table in front of her.

She sipped the drink, looked at the floor, didn't answer.

De Ruse looked back at the blond man. The three other men had made bets. The croupier looked impatient and at the same time watchful.

De Ruse said: "How come you always hit zero when I hit red, and double zero when I hit black?"

The blond young man smiled, shrugged, said nothing.

De Ruse put his hand down on the layout and said very softly: "I asked you a question, mister."

"Maybe I'm Jesse Livermore," the blond young man grunted. "I like to sell short."

"What is this—slow motion?" one of the other men snapped.

"Make your plays, please, gentlemen," the croupier said.

De Ruse looked at him, said: "Let it go."

The croupier spun the wheel left-handed, flicked the ball with the same hand the opposite way. His right hand rested on the edge of the table.

The ball stopped at black 28, next to zero. The blond man laughed. "Close," he said, "close."

De Ruse checked his chips, stacked them carefully. "I'm down six grand," he said. "It's a little raw, but I guess there's money in it. Who runs this clip joint?"

The croupier smiled slowly and stared straight into De Ruse's eyes. He asked quietly: "Did you say clip joint?"

De Ruse nodded. He didn't bother to answer.

"I thought you said clip joint," the croupier said, and moved one foot, put weight on it.

Three of the men who had been playing picked their chips up quickly and went over to a small bar in the corner of the room. They ordered drinks and leaned their backs against the wall by the bar, watching De Ruse and the croupier. The blond man stayed put and smiled sarcastically at De Ruse.

"Tsk, tsk," he said thoughtfully. "Your manners."

Francine Ley finished her drink and leaned her head back against the wall again. Her eyes came down and watched De Ruse furtively, under the long lashes.

A paneled door opened after a moment and a very big man with a black mustache and very rough black eyebrows came in. The croupier moved his eyes to him, then to De Ruse, pointing with his glance.

"Yes, I thought you said clip joint," he repeated tonelessly.

The big man drifted to De Ruse's elbow, touched him with his own elbow.

"Out," he said impassively.

The blond man grinned and put his hands in the pockets of his dark gray suit. The big man didn't look at him.

De Ruse glanced across the layout at the croupier and said: "I'll take back my six grand and call it a day."

"Out," the big man said wearily, jabbing his elbow into De Ruse's side.

The bald-headed croupier smiled politely.

"You," the big man said to De Ruse, "ain't goin' to get tough, are you?"

De Ruse looked at him with sarcastic surprise. "Well, well, the bouncer," he said softly. "Take him, Nicky."

The blond man took his right hand out of his pocket and swung it. The sap looked black and shiny under the bright lights. It hit the big man on the back of the head with a soft thud. The big man clawed at De Ruse, who stepped away from him quickly and took a gun out from under his arm. The big man clawed at the edge of the roulette table and fell heavily on the floor.

Francine Ley stood up and made a strangled sound in her throat.

The blond man skipped sidewise, whirled and looked at the bartender. The bartender put his hands on top of the bar. The three men who had been playing roulette looked very interested, but they didn't move.

De Ruse said: "The middle button on his right sleeve, Nicky. I think it's copper."

"Yeah." The blond man drifted around the end of the table putting the sap back in his pocket. He went close to the croupier and took hold of the middle of three buttons on his right cuff, jerked it hard. At the second jerk it came away and a thin wire followed it out of the sleeve.

"Correct," the blond man said casually, let the croupier's arm drop.

"I'll take my six grand now," De Ruse said. "Then we'll go talk to your boss."

The croupier nodded slowly and reached for the rack of chips beside the roulette table.

The big man on the floor didn't move. The blond man put his right hand behind his hip and took a .45 automatic out from inside his waistband at the back.

He swung it in his hand, smiling pleasantly around the room.

**8**

They went along a balcony that looked down over the dining room and the dance floor. The lisp of hot jazz came up to them from the lithe, swaying bodies of a high-yaller band. With the lisp of jazz came the smell of food and cigarette smoke and perspiration. The balcony was high and the scene down below had a patterned look, like an overhead camera shot.

The bald-headed croupier opened a door in the corner of the balcony and went through without looking back. The blond man De Ruse had called Nicky went after him. Then De Ruse and Francine Ley.

There was a short hall with a frosted light in the ceiling. The door at the end of that looked like painted metal. The croupier put a plump finger on the small push button at the side, rang it in a certain way. There was a buzzing noise like the sound of an electric door release. The croupier pushed on the edge and opened it.

Inside was a cheerful room, half den and half office. There was a grate fire and a green leather davenport at right angles to it, facing the door. A man sitting on the davenport put a newspaper down and looked up and his face suddenly got livid. He was a small man with a tight round head, a tight round dark face. He had little lightless black eyes like buttons of jet.

There was a big flat desk in the middle of the room and a very tall man stood at the end of it with a cocktail shaker in his hands. His head turned slowly and he looked over his shoulder at the four people who came into the room while his hands continued to agitate the cocktail shaker in gentle rhythm. He had a cavernous face with sunken eyes, loose grayish skin, and close-cropped reddish hair without shine or parting. A thin crisscross scar like a German *Mensur* scar showed on his left cheek.

The tall man put the cocktail shaker down and

turned his body around and stared at the croupier. The man on the davenport didn't move. There was a crouched tensity in his not moving.

The croupier said: "I think it's a stick-up. But I couldn't help myself. They sapped Big George."

The blond man smiled gaily and took his .45 out of his pocket. He pointed it at the floor.

"He thinks it's a stick-up," he said. "Wouldn't that positively slay you?"

De Ruse shut the heavy door. Francine Ley moved away from him, towards the side of the room away from the fire. He didn't look at her. The man on the davenport looked at her, looked at everybody.

De Ruse said quietly: "The tall one is Zapparty. The little one is Mops Parisi."

The blond man stepped to one side, leaving the croupier alone in the middle of the room. The .45 covered the man on the davenport.

"Sure, I'm Zapparty," the tall man said. He looked at De Ruse curiously for a moment.

Then he turned his back and picked the cocktail shaker up again, took out the plug and filled a shallow glass. He drained the glass, wiped his lips with a sheer lawn handkerchief and tucked the handkerchief back into his breast pocket very carefully, so that three points showed.

DeRuse smiled his thin metallic smile and touched one end of his left eyebrow with his forefinger. His right hand was in his jacket pocket.

"Nicky and I put on a little act," he said. "That was so the boys outside would have something to talk about if the going got too noisy when we came in to see you."

"It sounds interesting," Zapparty agreed. "What did you want to see me about?"

"About that gas car you take people for rides in," De Ruse said.

The man on the davenport made a very sudden movement and his hand jumped off his leg as if something had stung it. The blond man said: "No . . . or yes, if you'd rather, Mister Parisi. It's all a matter of taste."

Parisi became motionless again. His hand dropped back to his short thick thigh.

Zapparty widened his deep eyes a little. "Gas car?" His tone was of mild puzzlement.

De Ruse went forward into the middle of the room near the croupier. He stood balanced on the balls of his feet. His gray eyes had a sleepy glitter but his face was drawn and tired, not young.

He said: "Maybe somebody just tossed it in your lap, Zapparty, but I don't think so. I'm talking about the blue Lincoln, License 5A6, with the tank of Nevada gas in front. You know, Zapparty, the stuff they use on killers in our state."

Zapparty swallowed and his large Adam's apple moved in and out. He puffed his lips, then drew them back against his teeth, then puffed them again.

The man on the davenport laughed out loud, seemed to be enjoying himself.

A voice that came from no one in the room said sharply: "Just drop that gat, blondie. The rest of you grab air."

De Ruse looked up towards an opened panel in the wall beyond the desk. A gun showed in the opening, and a hand, but no body or face. Light from the room lit up the hand and the gun.

The gun seemed to point directly at Francine Ley. De Ruse said: "Okey," quickly, and lifted his hands, empty.

The blond man said: "That'll be Big George—all rested and ready to go." He opened his hand and let the .45 thud to the floor in front of him.

Parisi stood up very swiftly from the davenport and took a gun from under his arm. Zapparty took a revolver out of the desk drawer, leveled it. He spoke towards the panel: "Get out, and stay out."

The panel clicked shut. Zapparty jerked his head at

the bald-headed croupier, who had not seemed to move a muscle since he came into the room.

"Back on the job, Louis. Keep the chin up."

The croupier nodded and turned and went out of the room, closing the door carefully behind him.

Francine Ley laughed foolishly. Her hand went up and pulled the collar of her wrap close around her throat, as if it was cold in the room. But there were no windows and it was very warm, from the fire.

Parisi made a whistling sound with his lips and teeth and went quickly to De Ruse and stuck the gun he was holding in De Ruse's face, pushing his head back. He felt in De Ruse's pockets with his left hand, took the Colt, felt under his arms, circled around him, touched his hips, came to the front again.

He stepped back a little and hit De Ruse on the cheek with the flat of one gun. De Ruse stood perfectly still except that his head jerked a little when the hard metal hit his face.

Parisi hit him again the same place. Blood began to run down De Ruse's cheek from the cheekbone, lazily. His head sagged a little and his knees gave way. He went down slowly, leaned with his left hand on the floor, shaking his head. His body was crouched, his legs doubled under him. His right hand dangled loosely beside his left foot.

Zapparty said: "All right, Mops. Don't get blood-hungry. We want words out of these people."

Francine Ley laughed again, rather foolishly. She swayed along the wall, holding one hand up against it.

Parisi breathed hard and backed away from De Ruse with a happy smile on his round swart face.

"I been waitin' a long time for this," he said.

When he was about six feet from De Ruse something small and darkly glistening seemed to slide out of the left leg of De Ruse's trousers into his hand. There was a sharp, snapping explosion, a tiny orange-green flame down on the floor.

Parisi's head jerked back. A round hole appeared under his chin. It got large and red almost instantly. His hands opened laxly and the two guns fell out of them. His body began to sway. He fell heavily.

Zapparty said: "Holy Christ!" and jerked up his revolver.

Francine Ley screamed flatly and hurled herself at him—clawing, kicking, shrilling.

The revolver went off twice with a heavy crash. Two slugs plunked into a wall. Plaster rattled.

Francine Ley slid down to the floor, on her hands and knees. A long slim leg sprawled out from under her dress.

The blond man, down on one knee with his .45 in his hand again, rasped: "She got the bastard's gun!"

Zapparty stood with his hands empty, a terrible expression on his face. There was a long red scratch on the back of his right hand. His revolver lay on the floor beside Francine Ley. His horrified eyes looked down at it unbelievingly.

Parisi coughed once on the floor and after that was still.

De Ruse got up on his feet. The little Mauser looked like a toy in his hand. His voice seemed to come from far away saying: "Watch that panel, Nicky. . . ."

There was no sound outside the room, no sound anywhere. Zapparty stood at the end of the desk, frozen, ghastly.

De Ruse bent down and touched Francine Ley's shoulder. "All right, baby?"

She drew her legs under her and got up, stood looking down at Parisi. Her body shook with a nervous chill.

"I'm sorry, baby," De Ruse said softly beside her. "I guess I had a wrong idea about you."

He took a handkerchief out of his pocket and moistened it with his lips, then rubbed his left sheek lightly and looked at blood on the handkerchief.

Nicky said: "I guess Big George went to sleep again. I was a sap not to blast at him."

De Ruse nodded a little, and said:

"Yeah. The whole play was lousy. Where's your hat and coat, Mister Zapparty? We'd like to have you go riding with us."

## 9

In the shadows under the pepper trees De Ruse said: "There it is, Nicky. Over there. Nobody's bothered it. Better take a look around."

The blond man got out from under the wheel of the Packard and went off under the trees. He stood a little while on the same side of the street as the Packard, then he slipped across to where the big Lincoln was parked in front of the brick apartment house on North Kenmore.

De Ruse leaned forward across the back of the front seat and pinched Francine Ley's cheek. "You're going home now, baby—with this bus. I'll see you later."

"Johnny"—she clutched at his arm—"what are you going to do? For Pete's sake, can't you stop having fun for tonight?"

"Not yet, baby. Mister Zapparty wants to tell us things. I figure a little ride in that gas car will pep him up. Anyway I need it for evidence."

He looked sidewise at Zapparty in the corner of the back seat. Zapparty made a harsh sound in his throat and stared in front of him with a shadowed face.

Nicky came back across the road, stood with one foot on the running board.

"No keys," he said. "Got 'em?"

De Ruse said: "Sure." He took keys out of his pocket and handed them to Nicky. Nicky went around to Zapparty's side of the car and opened the door.

"Out, mister."

Zapparty got out stiffly, stood in the soft, slanting rain, his mouth working. De Ruse got out after him.

"Take it away, baby."

Francine Ley slid along the seat under the steering wheel of the Packard and pushed the starter. The motor caught with a soft whirr.

"So long, baby," De Ruse said gently. "Get my slippers warmed for me. And do me a big favor, honey. Don't phone anyone."

The Packard went off along the dark street, under the big pepper trees. De Ruse watched it turn a corner. He prodded Zapparty with his elbow.

"Let's go. You're going to ride in the back of your gas car. We can't feed you much gas on account of the hole in the glass, but you'll like the smell of it. We'll go off in the country somewhere. We've got all night to play with you."

"I guess you know this is a snatch," Zapparty said harshly.

"Don't I love to think it," De Ruse purred.

They went across the street, three men walking together without haste. Nicky opened the good rear door of the Lincoln. Zapparty got into it. Nicky banged the door shut, got under the wheel and fitted the ignition key in the lock. De Ruse got in beside him and sat with his legs straddling the tank of gas.

The whole car still smelled of the gas.

Nicky started the car, turned it in the middle of the block and drove north to Franklin, back over Los Feliz towards Glendale. After a little while Zapparty leaned forward and banged on the glass. De Ruse put his ear to the hole in the glass behind Nicky's head.

Zapparty's harsh voice said: "Stone house—Castle Road—in the La Crescenta flood area."

"Jeeze, but he's a softy," Nicky grunted, his eyes on the road ahead.

De Ruse nodded, said thoughtfully: "There's more to

it than that. With Parisi dead he'd clam up unless he figured he had an out."

Nicky said: "Me, I'd rather take a beating and keep my chin buttoned. Light me a pill, Johnny."

De Ruse lit two cigarettes and passed one to the blond man. He glanced back at Zapparty's long body in the corner of the car. Passing light touched up his taut face, made the shadows on it look very deep.

The big car slid noiselessly through Glendale and up the grade towards Montrose. From Montrose over to the Sunland highway and across that into the almost deserted flood area of La Crescenta.

They found Castle Road and followed it towards the mountains. In a few minutes they came to the stone house.

It stood back from the road, across a wide space which might once have been lawn but which was now packed sand, small stones and a few large boulders. The road made a square turn just before they came to it. Beyond it the road ended in a clean edge of concrete chewed off by the flood of New Year's Day, 1934.

Beyond this edge was the main wash of the flood. Bushes grew in it and there were many huge stones. On the very edge a tree grew with half its roots in the air eight feet above the bed of the wash.

Nicky stopped the car and turned off the lights and took a big nickeled flash out of the car pocket. He handed it to De Ruse.

De Ruse got out of the car and stood for a moment with his hand on the open door, holding the flash. He took a gun out of his overcoat pocket and held it down at his side.

"Looks like a stall," he said. "I don't think there's anything stirring here."

He glanced in at Zapparty, smiled sharply and walked off across the ridges of sand, towards the house. The front door stood half open, wedged that way by sand. De Ruse went towards the corner of the house, keeping out of line with the door as well as he could. He went along the side wall, looking at boarded-up windows behind which there was no trace of light.

At the back of the house was what had been a chicken house. A piece of rusted junk in a squashed garage was all that remained of the family sedan. The back door was nailed up like the windows. De Ruse stood silent in the rain, wondering why the front door was open. Then he remembered that there had been another flood a few months before, not such a bad one. There might have been enough water to break open the door on the side towards the mountains.

Two stucco houses, both abandoned, loomed on the adjoining lots. Farther away from the wash, on a bit of higher ground, there was a lighted window. It was the only light anywhere in the range of De Ruse's vision.

He went back to the front of the house and slipped through the open door, stood inside it and listened. After quite a long time he snapped the flash on.

The house didn't smell like a house. It smelled like out of doors. There was nothing in the front room but sand, a few pieces of smashed furniture, some marks on the walls, above the dark line of the flood water, where pictures had hung.

De Ruse went through a short hall into a kitchen that had a hole in the floor where the sink had been and a rusty gas stove stuck in the hole. From the kitchen he went into a bedroom. He had not heard any whisper of sound in the house so far.

The bedroom was square and dark. A carpet stiff with old mud was plastered to the floor. There was a metal bed with a rusted spring, and a waterstained mattress over part of the spring.

Feet stuck out from under the bed.

They were large feet in walnut brown brogues, with purple socks above them. The socks had gray clocks down the sides. Above the socks were trousers of black and white check.

De Ruse stood very still and played the flash down on the feet. He made a soft sucking sound with his lips. He stood like that for a couple of minutes, without moving at all. Then he stood the flash on the floor, on its end, so that the light it shot against the ceiling was reflected down to make dim light all over the room.

He took hold of the mattress and pulled it off the bed. He reached down and touched one of the hands of the man who was under the bed. The hand was ice cold. He took hold of the ankles and pulled, but the man was large and heavy.

It was easier to move the bed from over him.

## 10

Zapparty leaned his head back against the upholstery and shut his eyes and turned his head away a little. His eyes were shut very tight and he tried to turn his head far enough so that the light from the big flash wouldn't shine through his eyelids.

Nicky held the flash close to his face and snapped it on, off again, on, off again, monotonously, in a kind of rhythm.

De Ruse stood with one foot on the running board by the open door and looked off through the rain. On the edge of the murky horizon an airplane beacon flashed weakly.

Nicky said carelessly: "You never know what'll get a guy. I saw one break once because a cop held his fingernail against the dimple in his chin."

De Ruse laughed under his breath. "This one is tough," he said. "You'll have to think of something better than a flashlight."

Nicky snapped the flash on, off, on, off. "I could," he said, "But I don't want to get my hands dirty."

After a little while Zapparty raised his hands in front of him and let them fall slowly and began to talk. He talked in a low monotonous voice, keeping his eyes shut against the flash.

"Parisi worked the snatch. I didn't know anything about it until it was done. Parisi muscled in on me about a month ago, with a couple of tough boys to back him up. He had found out somehow that Candless beat me out of twenty-five grand to defend my half-brother on a murder rap, then sold the kid out. I didn't tell Parisi that. I didn't know he knew until tonight.

"He came into the club about seven or a little after and said: 'We've got a friend of yours, Hugo Candless. It's a hundred-grand job, a quick turnover. All you have to do is help spread the pay-off across the tables here, get it mixed up with a bunch of other money. You have to do that because we give you a cut—and because the caper is right up your alley, if anything goes sour.' That's about all. Parisi sat around then and chewed his fingers and waited for his boys. He got pretty jumpy when they didn't show. He went out once to make a phone call from a beer parlor."

De Ruse drew on a cigarette he held cupped inside a hand.

He said: "Who fingered the job, and how did you know Candless was up here?"

Zapparty said: "Mops told me. But I didn't know he was dead."

Nicky laughed and snapped the flash several times quickly.

De Ruse said: "Hold it steady for a minute."

Nicky held the beam steady on Zapparty's white face. Zapparty moved his lips in and out. He opened his eyes once. They were blind eyes, like the eyes of a dead fish.

Nicky said: "It's damn cold up here. What do we do with his nibs?"

De Ruse said: "We'll take him into the house and tie him to Candless. They can keep each other warm.

We'll come up again in the morning and see if he's got any fresh ideas."

Zapparty shuddered. The gleam of something like a tear showed in the corner of his nearest eye. After a moment of silence he said: "Okey. I planned the whole thing. The gas car was my idea. I didn't want the money. I wanted Candless, and I wanted him dead. My kid brother was hanged in Quentin a week ago Friday."

There was a little silence. Nicky said something under his breath. De Ruse didn't move or make a sound.

Zapparty went on: "Mattick, the Candless driver, was in on it. He hated Candless. He was supposed to drive the ringer car to make everything look good and then take a powder. But he lapped up too much corn getting set for the job and Parisi got leery of him, had him knocked off. Another boy drove the car. It was raining and that helped."

De Ruse said: "Better—but still not all of it, Zapparty."

Zapparty shrugged quickly, slightly opened his eyes against the flash, almost grinned.

"What the hell do you want? Jam on both sides?"

De Ruse said: "I want a finger put on the bird that had me grabbed . . . Let it go. I'll do it myself."

He took his foot off the running board and snapped his butt away into the darkness. He slammed the car door shut, got in the front. Nicky put the flash away and slid around under the wheel, started the engine.

De Ruse said: "Somewhere where I can phone for a cab, Nicky. Then you take this riding for another hour and then call Francy. I'll have a word for you there."

The blond man shook his head slowly from side to side. "You're a good pal, Johnny, and I like you. But this has gone far enough this way. I'm taking it down to Headquarters. Don't forget I've got a private-dick license under my old shirts at home."

De Ruse said: "Give me an hour, Nicky. Just an hour."

The car slid down the hill and crossed the Sunland Highway, started down another hill towards Montrose. After a while Nicky said: "Check."

# 11

It was twelve minutes past one by the stamping clock on the end of the desk in the lobby of the Casa de Oro. The lobby was antique Spanish, with black and red Indian rugs, nail-studded chairs with leather cushions and leather tassels on the corners of the cushions; the gray-green olivewood doors were fitted with clumsy wrought-iron strap hinges.

A thin, dapper clerk with a waxed blond mustache and a blond pompadour leaned on the desk and looked at the clock and yawned, tapping his teeth with the backs of his bright fingernails.

The door opened from the street and De Ruse came in. He took off his hat and shook it, put it on again and yanked the brim down. His eyes looked slowly around the deserted lobby and he went to the desk, slapped a gloved palm on it.

"What's the number of the Hugo Candless bungalow?" he asked.

The clerk looked annoyed. He glanced at the clock, at De Ruse's face, back at the clock. He smiled superciliously, spoke a slight accent.

"Twelve C. Do you wish to be announced—at this hour?"

De Ruse said: "No."

He turned away from the desk and went towards a large door with a diamond of glass in it. It looked like the door of a very high-class privy.

As he put his hand out to the door a bell rang sharply behind him.

De Ruse looked back over his shoulder, turned and went back to the desk. The clerk took his hand away from the bell, rather quickly.

His voice was cold, sarcastic, insolent, saying: "It's not that kind of apartment house, if you please."

Two patches above De Ruse's cheekbones got a dusky red. He leaned across the counter and took hold of the braided lapel of the clerk's jacket, pulled the man's chest against the edge of the desk.

"What was that crack, nance?"

The clerk paled but managed to bang his bell again with a flailing hand.

A pudgy man in a baggy suit and a seal-brown toupee came around the corner of the desk, put out a plump finger and said: "Hey."

De Ruse let the clerk go. He looked expressionlessly at cigar ash on the front of the pudgy man's coat.

The pudgy man said: "I'm the house man. You gotta see me if you want to get tough."

De Ruse said: "You speak my language. Come over in the corner."

They went over in the corner and sat down beside a palm. The pudgy man yawned amiably and lifted the edge of his toupee and scratched under it.

"I'm Kuvalick," he said. "Times I could bop that Swiss myself. What's the beef?"

De Ruse said: "Are you a guy that can stay clammed?"

"No. I like to talk. It's all the fun I get around this dude ranch." Kuvalick got half of a cigar out of a pocket and burned his nose lighting it.

De Ruse said: "This is one time you stay clammed."

He reached inside his coat, got his wallet out, took out two tens. He rolled them around his forefinger, then slipped them off in a tube and tucked the tube into the outside pocket of the pudgy man's coat.

Kuvalick blinked, but didn't say anything.

De Ruse said: "There's a man in the Candless apartment named George Dial. His car's outside, and that's where he would be. I want to see him and I don't want to send a name in. You can take me in and stay with me."

The pudgy man said cautiously: "It's kind of late. Maybe he's in bed."

"If he is, he's in the wrong bed," De Ruse said. "He ought to get up."

The pudgy man stood up. "I don't like what I'm thinkin', but I like your tens," he said. "I'll go in and see if they're up. You stay put."

De Ruse nooded. Kuvalick went along the wall and slipped through a door in the corner. The clumsy square butt of a hip holster showed under the back of his coat as he walked. The clerk looked after him, then looked contemptuously towards De Ruse and got out a nail file.

Ten minutes went by, fifteen. Kuvalick didn't come back. De Ruse stood up suddenly, scowled and marched towards the door in the corner. The clerk at the desk stiffened, and his eyes went to the telephone on the desk, but he didn't touch it.

De Ruse went through the door and found himself under a roofed gallery. Rain dripped softly off the slanting tiles of the roof. He went along a patio the middle of which was an oblong pool framed in a mosaic of gaily colored tiles. At the end of that, other patios branched off. There was a window light at the far end of the one to the left. He went towards it, at a venture, and when he came close to it made out the number 12C on the door.

He went up two flat steps and punched a bell that rang in the distance. Nothing happened. In a little while he rang again, then tried the door. It was locked. Somewhere inside he thought he heard a faint muffled thumping sound.

He stood in the rain a moment, then went around the corner of the bungalow, down a narrow, very wet passage to the back. He tried the service door; locked also. De Ruse swore, took his gun out from under his arm, held his hat against the glass panel of the service door and smashed the pane with the butt of the gun. Glass fell tinkling lightly inside.

He put the gun away, straightened his hat on his head and reached in through the broken pane to unlock the door.

The kitchen was large and bright with black and yellow tiling, looked as if it was used mostly for mixing drinks. Two bottles of Haig and Haig, a bottle of Hennessy, three or four kinds of fancy cordial bottles stood on the tiled drainboard. A short hall with a closed door led to the living room. There was a grand piano in the corner with a lamp lit beside it. Another lamp on a low table with drinks and glasses. A wood fire was dying on the hearth.

The thumping noise got louder.

De Ruse went across the living room and through a door framed in a valance into another hallway, thence into a beautifully paneled bedroom. The thumping noise came from a closet. De Ruse opened the door of the closet and saw a man.

He was sitting on the floor with his back in a forest of dresses on hangers. A towel was tied around his face. Another held his ankles together. His wrists were tied behind him. He was a very bald man, as bald as the croupier at the Club Egypt.

De Ruse stared down at him harshly, then suddenly grinned, bent and cut him loose.

The man spit a washcloth out of his mouth, swore hoarsely and dived into the clothes at the back of the closet. He came up with something furry clutched in his hand, straightened it out, and put it on his hairless head.

That made him Kuvalick, the house dick.

He got up still swearing and backed away from De

Ruse, with a stiff alert grin on his fat face. His right hand shot to his hip holster.

De Ruse spread his hands, said: "Tell it," and sat down in a small chintz-covered slipper chair.

Kuvalick stared at him quietly for a moment, then took his hand away from his gun.

"There's lights," he said, "So I push the buzzer. A tall dark guy opens. I seen him around here a lot. That's Dial. I say to him there's a guy outside in the lobby wants to see him hush-hush, won't give a name."

"That made you a sap," De Ruse commented dryly.

"Not yet, but soon," Kuvalick grinned, and spit a shred of cloth out of his mouth. "I describe you. *That* makes me a sap. He smiled kind of funny and asks me to come in a minute. I go in past him and he shuts the door and sticks a gun in my kidney. He says: 'Did you say he wore all dark clothes?' I say: 'Yes. And what's that gat for?' He says: 'Does he have gray eyes and sort of crinkly black hair and is he hard around the teeth?' I say: 'Yes, you bastard and what's the gat for?'

"He says: 'For this,' and lets me have it on the back of the head. I go down, groggy, but not out. Then the Candless broad comes out from a doorway and they tie me up and shove me in the closet and that's that. I hear them fussin' around for a little while and then I hear silence. That's all until you ring the bell."

De Ruse smiled lazily, pleasantly. His whole body was lax in the chair. His manner had become indolent and unhurried.

"They faded," he said softly. "They got tipped off. I don't think that was very bright."

Kuvalick said: "I'm an old Wells Fargo dick and I can stand a shock. What they been up to?"

"What kind of woman is Mrs. Candless?"

"Dark, a looker, Sex hungry, as the fellow says. Kind of worn and tight. They get a new chauffeur every three months. There's a couple guys in the Casa she likes too. I guess there's this gigolo that bopped me."

De Ruse looked at his watch, nodded, leaned forward to get up. "I guess it's about time for some law. Got any friends downtown you'd like to give a snatch story to?"

A voice said: "Not quite yet."

George Dial came quickly into the room from the hallway and stood quietly inside it with a long, thin, silenced automatic in his hand. His eyes were bright and mad, but his lemon-colored finger was very steady on the trigger of the small gun.

"We didn't fade," he said. "We weren't quite ready. But it might not have been a bad idea—for you two."

Kuvalick's pudgy hand swept for his hip holster.

The small automatic with the black tube on it made two flat dull sounds.

A puff of dust jumped from the front of Kuvalick's coat. His hands jerked sharply away from the sides and his small eyes snapped very wide open, like seeds bursting from a pod. He fell heavily on his side against the wall, lay quite still on his left side, with his eyes half open and his back against the wall. His toupee was tipped over rakishly.

De Ruse looked at him swiftly, looked back at Dial. No emotion showed in his face, not even excitement.

He said: "You're a crazy fool, Dial. That kills your last chance. You could have bluffed it out. But that's not your only mistake."

Dial said calmly: "No. I see that now. I shouldn't have sent the boys after you. I did that just for the hell of it. That comes of not being a professional."

De Ruse nodded slightly, looked at Dial almost with friendliness. "Just for the fun of it—who tipped you off the game had gone smash?"

"Francy—and she took her damn time about it," Dial said savagely. "I'm leaving, so I won't be able to thank her for a while."

"Not ever," De Ruse said. "You won't get out of the state. You won't ever touch a nickel of the big boy's money. Not you or your sidekicks or your woman. The cops are getting the story—right now."

Dial said: "We'll get clear. We have enough to tour Johnny. So long."

Dial's face tightened and his hand jerked up, with the gun in it. De Ruse half closed his eyes, braced himself for the shock. The little gun didn't go off. There was a rustle behind Dial and a tall dark woman in a gray fur coat slid into the room. A small hat was balanced on dark hair knotted on the nape of her neck. She was pretty, in a thin, haggard sort of way. The lip rouge on her mouth was as black as soot; there was no color in her cheeks.

She had a cool lazy voice that didn't match with her taut expression. "Who is Francy?" she asked coldly.

De Ruse opened his eyes wide and his body got stiff in the chair and his right hand began to slide up towards his chest.

"Francy is my girl friend," he said. "Mister Dial has been trying to get her away from me. But that's all right. He's a handsome lad and ought to be able to pick his spots."

The tall woman's face suddenly became dark and wild and furious. She grabbed fiercely at Dial's arm, the one that held the gun.

De Ruse snatched for his shoulder holster, got his .38 loose. But it wasn't his gun that went off. It wasn't the silenced automatic in Dial's hand. It was a huge frontier Colt with an eight-inch barrel and a boom like an exploding bomb. It went off from the floor, from beside Kuvalick's right hip, where Kuvalick's plump hand held it.

It went off just once. Dial was thrown back against the wall as if by a giant hand. His head crashed against the wall and instantly his darkly handsome face was a mask of blood.

He fell laxly down the wall and the little automatic with the black tube on it fell in front of him. The dark woman dived for it, down on her hands and knees in front of Dial's sprawled body.

She got it, began to bring it up. Her face was convulsed, her lips were drawn back over thin wolfish teeth that shimmered.

Kuvalick's voice said: "I'm a tough guy. I used to be a Wells Fargo dick."

His great cannon slammed again. A shrill scream was torn from the woman's lips. Her body was flung against Dial's. Her eyes opened and shut, opened and shut. Her face got white and vacant.

"Shoulder shot. She's okay," Kuvalick said, and got up on his feet. He jerked open his coat and patted his chest.

"Bullet-proof vest," he said proudly. "But I thought I'd better lie quiet for a while or he'd popped me in the face."

## 12

Francine Ley yawned and stretched out a long green pajama-clad leg and looked at a slim green slipper on her bare foot. She yawned again, got up and walked nervously across the room to the kidney-shaped desk. She poured a drink, drank it quickly, with a sharp nervous shudder. Her face was drawn and tired, her eyes hollow; there were dark smudges under her eyes.

She looked at the tiny watch on her wrist. It was almost four o'clock in the morning. Still with her wrist up she whirled at a sound, put her back to the desk and began to breathe very quickly, pantingly.

De Ruse came in through the red curtains. He stopped and looked at her without expression, then slowly took off his hat and overcoat and dropped them on a chair. He took off his suit coat and his tan shoulder harness and walked over to the drinks.

He sniffed at a glass, filled it a third full of whiskey, put it down in a gulp.

"So you had to tip the louse off," he said somberly, looking down into the empty glass he held.

Francine Ley said: "Yes. I had to phone him. What happened?"

"You had to phone the louse," De Ruse said in exactly the same tone. "You knew damn well he was mixed up in it. You'd rather he got loose, even if he cooled me off doing it."

"You're all right, Johnny?" She asked softly, tiredly.

DeRuse didn't speak, didn't look at her. He put the glass down slowly and poured some more whiskey into it, added charged water, looked around for some ice. Not finding any he began to sip the drink with his eyes on the white top of the desk.

Francine Ley said: "There isn't a guy in the world that doesn't rate a start on you, Johnny. It wouldn't do him any good, but he'd have to have it, if I knew him."

De Ruse said slowly: "That's swell. Only I'm not quite that good. I'd be a stiff right now except for a comic hotel dick that wears a Buntline Special and a bullet-proof vest to work."

After a little while Francine Ley said: "Do you want me to blow?"

De Ruse looked at her quickly, looked away again. He put his glass down and walked away from the desk. Over his shoulder he said: "Not so long as you keep on telling me the truth."

He sat down in a deep chair and leaned his elbows on the arms of it, cupped his face in his hands. Francine Ley watched him for a moment, then went over and sat on an arm of the chair. She pulled his head back gently until it was against the back of the chair. She began to stroke his forehead.

De Ruse closed his eyes. His body became loose and relaxed. His voice began to sound sleepy.

"You saved my life over at the Club Egypt maybe. I

guess that gave you the right to let handsome have a shot at me."

Francine Ley stroked his head, without speaking.

"Handsome is dead," De Ruse went on. "The peeper shot his face off."

Francine Ley's hand stopped. In a moment it began again, stroking his head.

"The Candless frau was in on it. Seems she's a hot number. She wanted Hugo's dough, and she wanted all the men in the world except Hugo. Thank heaven she didn't get bumped. She talked plenty. So did Zapparty."

"Yes, honey," Francine Ley said quietly.

De Ruse yawned. "Candless is dead. He was dead before we started. They never wanted him anything else but dead. Parisi didn't care one way or the other, as long as he got paid."

Francine Ley said: "Yes, honey."

"Tell you the rest in the morning," De Ruse said thickly. "I guess Nicky and I are all square with the law . . . Let's go to Reno, get married . . . I'm sick of this tomcat life . . . Get me 'nother drink, baby."

Francine Ley didn't move except to draw her fingers softly and soothingly across his forehead and back over his temples. De Ruse moved lower in the chair. His head rolled to one side.

"Yes, honey."

"Don't call me honey," De Ruse said thickly. "Just call me pigeon."

When he was quite asleep she got off the arm of the chair and went and sat down near him. She sat very still and watched him, her face cupped in her long delicate hands with the cherry-colored nails.

## About the Author

RAYMOND CHANDLER was born in Chicago, Illinois, on July 23, 1888, but spent most of his boyhood and youth in England, where he attended Dulwich College and later worked as a free-lance journalist for *The Westminster Gazette* and *The Spectator*. During World War I, he served in France with the First Division of the Canadian Expeditionary Force, transferring later to the Royal Flying Corps (R.A.F.). In 1919 he returned to the United States, settling in California, where he eventually became director of a number of independent oil companies. The Depression put an end to his business career, and in 1933, at the age of forty-five, he turned to writing, publishing his first stories in *Black Mask*. His first novel, *The Big Sleep,* was published in 1939. Never a prolific writer, he published only one collection of stories and seven novels in his lifetime. In the last year of his life he was elected president of the Mystery Writers of America. He died in La Jolla, California, on March 26, 1959.

About the Author

RAYMOND CHANDLER was born in Chicago, Illinois, in 1888, but spent much of his boyhood
and youth in England, where he attended Dulwich College.
He returned later, settled in California, and worked as a
bookkeeper and journalist. He was in his forties when he
began writing detective fiction as a career. His first novel,
*The Big Sleep*, was published in 1939. He went on to write
*Farewell, My Lovely*, *The Lady in the Lake*, and other books.
He died in La Jolla, California, in 1959.

# KEEP YOURSELF IN
# *SUSPENSE...*
## from
# BALLANTINE BOOKS